ALTERNATIVE ALAMAT

MELU

ALTERNATIVE ALAMAT

Myths and Legends From the Philippines

An Anthology

**edited by
Paolo Chikiamco**

TUTTLE Publishing

Tokyo | Rutland, Vermont | Singapore

Table of Contents

Acknowledgments

"Beneath the Acacia" © 2007/2011 by Celestine Trinidad. First appeared in *The Digest of Philippine Genre Stories Volume 1, Issue 2*, edited by Kenneth Yu (Kenneth Yu: Philippines).

"Keeper of My Sky" © 2010/2011 by Timothy James Dimacali. First appeared in *Philippine Speculative Fiction Volume 5* edited by Vincent Michael Simbulan and Nikki Alfar (Kestrel IMC: Philippines).

"Offerings to Aman Sinaya" © 2011 by Andrei Tupaz. First appeared in *Philippine Speculative Fiction Volume 6* edited by Nikki Alfar and Kate Osias (Kestrel IMC: Philippines).

For Shaps, Meia, and Kaito.

For my mother.

For all the stories that we've lived, and
all the horizons we will cross.

Preface to the International Edition

You hold in your hands a time capsule of sorts. The original edition of this anthology was published as an ebook in 2011, then a slightly expanded edition was released in print in the Philippines in 2014. Even with a gap of just three years, at the time it was hard to resist the urge to make substantial changes to the book . . . but if there's one thing I've learned as a writer, it's that there needs to be a point where you consider a work to be finished. So, while I did add bonus content to the print edition, I left the original manuscript largely unchanged. I've made the same decision for this international edition (except for the research guide), even if the urge to change things is much stronger when looking at text I wrote a decade ago.

Ten years . . . a lot has changed in that time span: for me and the contributors to the anthology; for the world and society at large. I write this while my country is still battling the COVID-19 pandemic, balancing on the razor's edge between lockdowns and re-openings. Just in the past two years we've seen so many things that would have been inconceivable not too long ago, and those of us fortunate enough to have made it to this point have had to adapt in order to survive.

In a sense, it's the same with the gods and heroes of old. They come from a time far different from our own, and for them to live again in the hearts and minds of those of us in the present, their stories must be retold—and in each new telling, with each new audience, those stories change. The gods adapt, when new voices say their names. The gods adapt,

9

when they are embodied in new forms. The gods change, and so they survive.

At the core of this anthology is the tension between old and new. They are re-tellings of myths, re-imaginings of old gods . . . but the anthology itself is a decade old now, and the world around it so different. But every story is new when read the first time, and as this edition reaches shores we never could before, I can't wait to see how our stories change, and how our gods survive.

—Paolo Chikiamco

Introduction

"For the educated [Filipino] minority, Greek and Roman mythology is more familiar than their own. They can summon Apollo and Aphrodite or mentally wander around Olympus; but they are puzzled by Bugan and the seven levels of the Bukidnon sky-world. A vast area of our collective self, a self that is the product of generations of reflection upon life's meaning, is thus submerged in darkness. In fact, the ridges and valleys of this unexplored self continue to underlie our own view of the world, 'modern' though we are. A rediscovery of our myths unlocks this hidden continent."

—"The Soul Book" by Francisco Demetrio, Gilda Cordero-Fernando, and Fernando Zialcita

In one sense, to speak of Philippine mythology is to use a term of convenience. We are a nation of many indigenous cultures—numbering anywhere from sixty to over a hundred, depending on who you ask—with distinct oral traditions. This makes learning about our mythology somewhat more difficult than would be the case for other nations, but it also gives us a cumulative heritage that is rich and diverse.

There is a dual beauty to Philippine mythology: the stories that we know, and the stories that we don't. From the former we gain gods of calamity and baldness, of cosmic time and lost things; we gain the bloodthirsty Banna, the lustful Labaw Donggon, the immortal Mungan; we gain the many-layered Skyworld, and weapons that fight their own battles; we gain a ship that is pulled to paradise by a chain, and a giant crab that controls the tides. These are ideas and images which inspire.

And yet, the stories we don't know are just as fascinating. Philippine mythology is rife with those unfilled spaces that kindle the imagination, "those marginal regions named and labeled", as Michael Chabon once put it. In some cases, all we have are fragments of a longer tale (as in the case of the Ibalon). In others, all that remains are the names of the gods and their divine functions, beautiful names and evocative duties, leaving us to wonder about the tales they once populated.

But here's the thing: when writers are inspired, when writers wonder, they write. This anthology is a product of that wonder and inspiration.

Within these pages, you won't find straight retellings of old tales—"alamat" is the Filipino word for "legend", and I've deliberately asked for stories that provide for "alternative" takes. Some stories build on what we know, or reexamine underlying assumptions. Others use names as catalysts, or play within the spaces where the myths are silent. What you will find in all these eleven stories, however, is a love for the myths, epics, and legends that reflect us, contain us, call to us.

In case the stories in this anthology whet your appetite for information about Philippine mythology, I've also included supplementary material in the form of interviews with experts in folklore and anthropology, as well as a rundown of notable Philippine gods and goddesses not featured in the anthology (interpreted visually by Mervin Malonzo in between the stories). This barely scratches the surface, of course, so you'll also find a brief survey of other resources at the end of the book.

"The gods," says Roberto Calasso in *Literature and the Gods*, "are fugitive guests of literature. They cross it with the trail of their names and are soon gone. Every time the writer sets down a word, he must fight to win them back." I hope that the stories in this volume will help to make them more frequent visitors.

—Paolo Chikiamco

BALITOK

Ana's Little Pawnshop on Makiling St.

Eliza Victoria

Eliza Victoria was born in 1986. Her fiction and poetry have received Carlos Palanca Memorial Awards for Literature and the Philippines Free Press Literary Awards. For additional information, visit her website at sungazer.wordpress.com.

Maria Makiling is one of the most popular figures in Philippine mythology, and she'll make more than one appearance in this anthology. In this story, however, she takes a back seat to one of the most obscure of our goddesses, one who also happens to reign over one of the most intriguing dominions.

"Tala used to own this pair."

Ana held up a pair of spectacles for me to see. The oval lenses were framed in glass filled with nebulae, turning a rich mauve-blue one moment, a bright golden-green the next. Every now and then stars formed, twinkling and floating around the lenses and toward the temple arms.

"Lisa would love that," I said. Lisa was my girlfriend. She got her first pair of prescription glasses two weeks ago, just a simple pair, framed in black, square and serious. She said the glasses made her look like a dork. I wondered if lenses framed by star-forming clouds would make her look like less of a dork. Probably not.

"I'll give this pair to you in exchange for your most treasured memory of the night sky," Ana said.

I had several. My top choices: That meteor shower last February, with Lisa beside me, sitting open-mouthed and speechless; or my clear view of the night sky in Bohol, as we lay in the sand, momentarily forgetting the impending end of summer vacation.

"No thanks," I said, smiling as I remembered.

"Good for you," Ana said.

I almost asked what Tala's eye grade was, but then realized that an entity that oversaw all the stars of the universe probably had perfect vision.

"Tala gave it to me in exchange for *this*."

This came out as a grunt as Ana leaned sideways to pick up another item. "The Mask of Alunsina," Ana said. "Tala said she'll have someone pick it up for her today." It was a golden half-mask with a handle, and covered in garnet, sapphire, and amethyst. Ana brought it to her face, and the mask turned the soft pink and yellow of dawn.

My jaw dropped. "Wow."

"Wow, indeed," Ana said, cradling the mask in her hands. "I think Tala underpaid me in this deal." She laughed.

"What did Alunsina get for it?"

"A good night's sleep," Ana said. "She just wanted to get rid of the thing. It bored her. Alunsina gets bored a lot, ever since she relinquished the realm of the golden dawn and became a mortal. She said it's hard to be too aware of the passage of time. The minutes now weigh on her, when, before, she could feel a century pass in the blink of an eye."

"She should have an Internet connection at her house," I said.

Ana found that hilarious. "I'll tell her that when she drops by. Can you hand me that box, please, Eric?"

I came upon Ana's little pawnshop by accident a month ago, when I was looking for a gift I had lost. It was hours after school, and I had left the bookstore with an expensive fountain pen that my father wanted for his birthday. I was so busy speeding down the road to reach home in time for dinner that I didn't realize I had lost my gift until I happened to touch my breast pocket. I got off my bike and walked back, retracing my path. Thank goodness I'd just passed a high-end residential street, quiet and cozy, the houses all elegant and expensive and bordered by flower gardens, and not some dark alley where I could lose things other than a blasted pen. I think I passed by a group of boys playing basketball, but I had my eyes trained on the ground, so I only heard their voices and the thump and clink of the ball as it hit the pavement and, occasionally, the ring.

All of a sudden the sounds disappeared. I looked up in surprise and found myself on a stretch of road lined with quaint little shops. One sold secondhand books; another, dresses and jewelry; and still another, lamps and chandeliers. All of them were closed, however, except for this one store lit by a yellow light from inside.

"Lost something?" a woman said. That was the first time I saw Ana. She seemed to be in her thirties and looked breathtakingly beautiful, her lines as defined as the stars in those forties-era films that Lisa liked so much: dark lids, red lips, wavy hair. And yet there was also something very warm about her presence. If this were actually a movie, I'd cast her as the hot aunt who didn't have children of her own, but who would have made an excellent mother.

I found myself saying, "I lost a pen."

"Ah," Ana said. She was in the process of moving a large

flowerpot closer to the door. The flowerpot contained the biggest sunflowers I had ever seen. She straightened up and wiped her palms on the side of her jeans before going inside. Her shop had a display window, behind which a hand-painted sign rested on a stand and read, "*Ana's Pawnshop*". Taped right on the glass was an announcement written with a black Sharpie: (1) ASSISTANT NEEDED. PART-TIME OR FULL-TIME.

I moved closer and settled my bike right beside the flowerpot. The pawnshop was cluttered but looked snug and warm, with its gleaming hardwood floors and a certain syrupy smell in the air. Ana was already behind the glass counter. At her elbow was a wicker basket filled with letters. All of the letters were unopened, sealed with moss-green wax bearing two intertwined M's. On the other side of the counter was a bare table with two chairs.

"Is this it?" In her hands was a rectangular box with a silver bow.

"Yes," I said in wonder. "How did that get here?"

"Lost things arrive here to be found," she said.

"Oh," I said. "Do I have to pay for this?"

"No," she said with a laugh. "I only sell the unclaimed items."

I looked at the shelves. "That's a lot of unclaimed items."

Ana looked wistful. "People lose things every day. Most just give up looking and forget."

I was curious about the shop and the sudden sadness in Ana's voice, but I was pressed for time, so I just thanked her and said goodbye.

(It must be mentioned, though, that despite the time I spent looking for the pen on that street, and the time I spent inside Ana's shop, I still arrived home in time for dinner.)

I went to the pawnshop again the next day, and I ended up staying there for at least an hour, having tea, eating bread, and looking over her inventory. Her tea (she said) was made from the boiled petals of *rosas*, *gumamela* and *sampaguita*, and was incredibly sweet and refreshing. I was sure she used ingredients besides the flowers; if I were to boil the exact same petals I would just end up with something foul and slimy.

Ana told me that lost objects appeared in the storeroom behind the shop, located beside Ana's kitchen and her bathroom (she slept in a bedroom upstairs), and would remain there until claimed. If the items remained unclaimed for thirty days, they would be moved to the shop to be appraised and sold.

The shop had all sorts of things: Wineglasses and mugs, magnifying glasses and spectacles and sunglasses of all shapes and sizes and colors, tables and chairs from various eras, curtains and clothes and bags and purses, typewriters, cameras, shoes and boots and pumps, chests of jewelry, musical boxes, dolls and other toys, lace and silk, bronze candelabras, combs inlaid with pearls, hats adorned with hand-sewn designs and rhinestones, large vintage buttons, books and notes and letters.

"My human clientele look through the shelves for items they can use as décor," Ana said. "Some of these things are too old and broken to be worn or used. They pay me with human currency, and that's what I use to pay the humans who come in to pawn their products. My non-human clientele, on the other hand, usually just end up bartering each other's items. They have no use for human objects, and humans more often than not refuse to pay the price I ask for the items of magic."

"Is this an orientation?" I asked, and Ana looked at me in surprise, and burst out laughing.

I knew before we finished our tea that I would ask about the sign taped on the display window, that she would (perhaps jokingly) ask me to apply, and I would pretend to consider, then I'd apply and she would say yes. And this was exactly what happened.

I only worked after school because I spent the weekend with Lisa (and Ana understood that). I never had the need to have a part-time job, but for a first part-time job, working with Ana was a pleasure. I liked Ana; she was nice, sincere, and I could taste her loneliness in the very bread she served.

Ana didn't really need a helper either. It wasn't like clients came in droves. But she only had her books and she couldn't understand the appeal of TV or radio. She was hungry for constant company.

My schedule was like this: school, have lunch with Lisa, extra-curricular shit (through Lisa's clever maneuvering, I found myself signing up for the school paper, and now I couldn't find a way out *anywhere*), say goodbye to Lisa, change out of my uniform, go to Ana's shop. That would be around four, so I'd arrive in time for tea and bread, then I would clean up, check the storeroom for new items, and help Ana move the heavier objects around the shop.

Ana opened her shop late, because clients usually came in at night, like nocturnal bingers prowling a convenience store for their chocolate fix. There was always the usual pawnshop business of this-wristwatch-for-cash, but I had also seen my share of interesting trades. A blind girl exchanging her singing voice for sight (Ana stored the girl's voice in a jar and placed it on the topmost shelf), a basketball player exchanging a week's worth of laughter for the quick mending of a broken bone. There was one night when a man came in and bought a bottle of storm clouds. He claimed to be a poet.

"I needed the rain," he said. "I couldn't write in this goddamn heat."

"What did he pay for that?" I asked, once the man had left.

"That's just a week's supply of storm clouds," Ana said, "so I only asked for six months of his life. I'm going to use that for my sunflowers. That way, they won't wilt for a long time—isn't that fantastic?"

I hoped the man wrote good poems.

Ana also had a lot of visitors, mortals and immortals alike. I was there when Alunsina banged in, wearing a short black dress and dark sunglasses, and smelling of acrylic. "A human!" she said when she saw me. "How interesting."

I wondered about the sunglasses. It was six in the evening.

Ana embraced her and arranged their teacups on the small table. Alunsina was asking about the mask. "So who finally bought the damn thing?"

"Tala did."

"*Tala?*" Alunsina burst out laughing. "Where will she use it?"

"It's a good accessory for an evening gown," Ana said.

"What, she'll throw a party? Good grief." She turned to me, and I realized that it wasn't acrylic wafting off of her—it was cheap gin. "Hey, if Tala ever invites you to her party, don't go. She's as dull as a dying galaxy."

I didn't have first-hand experience, obviously, but I was pretty sure a dying galaxy would be anything but dull. I believed it would be fantastic, breathtaking, heartbreaking. Not dull. But ex-immortal or no, Alunsina was drunk and seemed unstable, so I just nodded my head.

Alunsina's gaze strayed toward Ana's wicker basket of unopened letters. "Ohhh," she said. "Is the queen giving you a hard time?"

Ana sighed. "I bet they're strongly worded missives regarding my refusal to become a stockholder," Ana said. "I'm happy with my small shop. I don't need dividends."

"You shouldn't have trusted her," Alunsina said. "She's

corporate now. She'll screw you over one of these days."

"Sorry about that," Ana said, after having seen Alunsina out the door.

"Who's the queen?" I asked.

Ana looked at me a moment, then smiled and shook her head.

"Sorry," I said, my face reddening. "I couldn't help over-hearing—"

"Alunsina and her big mouth," Ana said, laughing. "It's all right, Eric. Who *is* the queen? I own this shop, but the rest of the block is owned by Mariang Makiling."

"I see," I said. "But doesn't she live in a forest?"

"This is the forest!" Ana said, gleeful, as though she had caught me in a trap. "Was. We're sitting right in it. A corporation bought the land from the government, tore down the trees, burned the grass, and filled it with cement and buildings. Instead of hurling curses all around, however, Mariang Makiling simply dusted herself off and struck a deal with the mortals. So now she's a stockholder and a businesswoman. I believe she now responds to 'Marie'." Ana shrugged. "I don't blame the poor girl. She's suffered through a string of heartbreaks. If she believes she can heal by jumping into finance, then good for her. I just hate how the business has affected her, how she now treasures the impersonal. She's been sending me letters instead of coming here to have tea with me." She shrugged and waved a hand toward the wicker basket, as though she wanted to banish it away from her sight.

Ana shifted topics. "Did you think what Tala gave me in exchange for her mask was useless?"

Alunsina had been berating her about it. "No," I said. "I think those are a really cool pair of glasses."

"Yes, but I've broken the frame." Ana took out a jar sealed with a black rubber cover. The contents of the jar sparkled.

"I've poured the nebulae here. They've been busy. Look how many stars they've made!"

I peered at them and smiled and nodded my approval.

I wanted to ask her why she bought the shop in the first place, but it seemed that every time I planned to ask her, Ana would talk about something else, deftly changing the subject.

Until, that is, the night I began yammering on about this little girl who went missing. Like I said, Ana didn't own a TV, and she didn't seem particularly interested in the newspapers, but it was all over the news and one moment I just found myself talking to her about it. The girl had last been seen leaving her kindergarten class with her *yaya*.

While watching the report, my mother mentioned another girl who had disappeared years ago. It was the same scenario: last seen with the *yaya* leaving school. A day later, they found the girl's shoes in the playground. Little pink shoes with straps and silver buckles. The girl had been missing for close to a week by then. No calls, no ransom demands. They couldn't find the *yaya*, either. Just those pink shoes.

"She was found dead inside a Samsonite bag three months after," I said. "The bag was fished from a river."

"How horrible," Ana said. "I hope the new missing girl won't end up the same way."

"Yes."

Silence.

"Have you had a person suddenly appear in the storeroom?" I asked.

"A person?"

"Humans get lost, too," I said. I imagined the little girl suddenly appearing in the storeroom, bewildered but safe.

"I deal with lost things," said Ana. "Lost humans are beyond my realm."

I thought that was the end of it, so I just nodded and busied myself with the inventory list.

"I've lost a little girl, too," Ana said, all of a sudden.

I was so surprised I didn't manage to say anything.

"But, no. She's not really lost." Ana wiped her palms on her jeans, watching her hands as she did so. "My, I'm an awful storyteller. Let me start again," she said. "I fell in love."

Ana was still Anagolay then, she said. She visited the world and fell in love with a mortal, and gave birth to a girl and lived as a married woman and a mother for years. But the man fell out of love, and Anagolay found herself abandoned.

"We met in this town, but he has moved away," Ana said. "I decided to stay here because I have fallen in love with the place, and there is still that faint hope that he'll come back. Maybe then he'll explain why he did what he did." Ana gave me a sad, resigned smile. "He took our daughter with him, when he left me."

"That's awful," I said. I almost asked for the man's name. I thought maybe I could Google him.

As though reading my mind, Ana said, "I tried looking for them. But then I thought, if I find them, *what then?* What use is it, to find people that don't want to be found? They're not lost: one decided to remove himself from my world, one was taken away. Better if I wait for them to come to me.

"So when I heard about Mariang Makiling's business endeavors, I visited her in her office and asked if I could be given a piece of land in this realm. I paid a portion of my influence for a small shop and her protection. With her glamour protecting this property, this is definitely the safest spot in town. In here you need not worry about fire, or floods, or the sort of evil that forces men to throw a dead child into a river. I can sleep soundly with the front door unlocked. It's a good deal. I run my shop, and I sit here and wait."

If the missing girl's mother knew this, she would have bought protection for her child in a heartbeat. I would. I would buy protection for my family. For Lisa.

But Mariang Makiling asked for a high price in return, and I didn't have powers to barter.

The letters bearing Mariang Makiling's seal kept ending up inside the wicker basket. More than once I was tempted to open one of them, but I kept my hands to myself and did my work without saying anything.

One day, a man in a suit dropped by the pawnshop. I had just arrived and wasn't even done putting butter on my bread when the little bell on top of the door tinkled. I thought we had an early customer.

"Greetings, Anagolay," the man said.

"Greetings, Michael," Ana said, rising. "But please, call me Ana. Eric," she said, turning to me, "would you mind it so much if you moved to the counter?"

We were sitting at the table. "No prob," I said, and took my tea with me.

I saw Michael glance at the wicker basket and sigh. "I see you haven't read any of Marie's letters."

Ana sat down again. "I don't want to become a stockholder," she said, a bit grumpily. "And I came to Mariang Makiling when I bought this shop. Would it be too much if she showed courtesy and came to me?"

"Don't take it that way," Michael said. "She's really, really busy. And the letters aren't about the stockholding issue."

"Then what does she want?"

"They're tearing down the building, Ana," Michael said. "Marie's human partners want to build a mall."

I almost choked on my tea.

"And she's allowing this?" Ana said. This was the first time

I saw her look so distraught. "But I own this shop."

"Yes, we'll provide you with another venue. But you'll have to pack up and leave by tomorrow. We had given you several months, but you never opened the letters and you never replied."

Ana chewed on this. Then: "Let me speak with Mariang Makiling."

Michael placed his briefcase on his lap and said, "I really just came here to present you with the documents—"

"Tell her. To come here."

Michael sighed. "Very well," he said, and dialed a number on his cell phone.

I didn't hear Michael talk to anyone on the other line, but he suddenly told us, "She's here," and the glass door banged open and in strode a woman in a white business suit and red pumps, followed by two female assistants and another man in a suit. The woman, who had long ebony hair and light-brown skin, looked stern and no-nonsense, and crossed her arms as though she would rather be elsewhere. Her assistants looked bored, as though unimpressed with the pawnshop's display. The other man in a suit, probably her bodyguard, was wearing sunglasses and looked like he couldn't care less about anyone else.

Mariang Makiling flipped her hair over a shoulder, and the shop was suddenly filled with the heady scent of *sampaguita*.

"Greetings, Maria," Ana said, and Mariang Makiling slumped her shoulders, smiled, and drew Ana closer for an embrace. I thought even this sudden friendliness was artificial.

"Greetings Anagolay," she said. "I assume Michael had told you the news."

"Is there no way I could keep my shop?"

"You *will* keep your shop, Anagolay. We'll just relocate you."

"Where? Somewhere near?"

Mariang Makiling didn't reply.

"I am sure," Ana said, "that you could let your mortals build this mall or whatever-it-is around me. I paid for this space dearly, Mariang Makiling. I paid for protection."

That got to her. Mariang Makiling placed her hands on her hips and took a deep breath. Her female assistants typed on their Blackberry's, Michael sighed and fidgeted, and the bodyguard stood as still as a sentinel.

"All the memories of your life's greatest love," Mariang Makiling said after that long pause, "and you can keep your shop."

Ana received the blow as gracefully as she could. "That would include memories of my daughter, Maria."

"So be it," Mariang Makiling said. "Consider my terms, Anagolay. I have a business to run."

And so they left. Only Michael looked apologetic. Ana only said, "Well", and nothing else, and I left her with her silence.

Then it was time to leave. As I was picking up my backpack Ana tapped me on the shoulder. I turned, and I felt a jar shoved into my hands.

"It's a gift," she said. "I believe Lisa will like it."

It was the jar containing the nebulae from Tala's spectacles, the star-forming clouds that I had admired but for which I refused to give up my night sky memories. Ana had tied a red bow around the lid, and attached a card that said, *To Eric and Lisa, from a dear friend.*

"Don't do it," I said.

Ana looked surprised. "Don't do what, Eric?"

"Don't give her what she asks for. Just relocate. If it's protection that worries you, buy locks, buy a stun gun or a bat, buy a proper cash register. I'll help you! Don't give her what she wants."

But that was all in my head. All I really said was: "Are you going to move?"

Ana smiled. "I haven't decided yet," she said. "I wonder, though: if somebody asked you to part with your unpleasant memories, wouldn't you say yes?"

"But your memories with your husband and daughter couldn't be all bad," I said.

"I know," Ana said. "That's the tricky part."

There was silence as I put the jar carefully in my backpack. "Will I see you tomorrow?" I asked.

But it was as though Ana didn't hear me. "Good night, Eric," she said. "Take care."

What else could I say? "Good night, Ana."

I walked out the door and heard the familiar tinkle of the bell. I looked back as I moved my bike. Ana, nestled in that yellow glow, smiled and waved goodbye from behind the glass door. I smiled back, gave her a salute, and pedaled away, the jar inside my bag quickly filling with stars.

BANGUNBANGUN

Harinuo's Love Song

Rochita Loenen-Ruiz

Rochita Loenen-Ruiz attended the Clarion West Writer's Workshop in 2009 as that year's Octavia Butler Scholar. Her work has been published in print and online, both abroad as well as in the Philippines. Some of the publications she has appeared in are: Weird Tales Magazine, Fantasy Magazine, Apex Magazine, and the Philippine Speculative Fiction Anthology (second and fourth volumes). She has stories coming out in the Second Apex Book of World SF and Realms of Fantasy. She is currently working on a tribal sf novel.

The myth of the Sky Maiden appears, in one form or another, in many cultures around the world. However, like many myths, when one peels back the surface of the story, strips it of the distancing devices of archetype and tradition, there are horrors to be found within. This story explores that horror, while mixing Mangyan poetry with Ifugao culture.

Harinuo. Eldest son of Andares Nawotwot. Born to hunt, born with dreams in his veins.

Harinuo. Four feet tall. Bare footed and thick soled from years of clambering up and down the mountain paths. Skin like polished mahogany, hair cropped close to the crown of his head.

Harinuo bowing before the chieftain of his tribe, laying his neck bare as an offering, in that one gesture saying, "all that I am, all I will be, is in your hands, my Chief."

Chief Agusan grunts and nods, takes the bow from the young man's hand and slides it across Harinuo's neck as an acknowledgement of this young man's desire to rise above his lowly station. A collective sigh rises from the tribe. It echoes the sigh escaping the young man's lips.

Now, the Mumbaki approaches holding out the dreaming cone. Every man, every hunter, every traveler remembers this from their own rite of passage. They know, one can never be full-fledged until he or she returns with a sight or a vision or a wisdom taken from the father of stars. Harinuo cannot return until he has taken for himself a spirit guide to stand guard at the portals of his house.

"Harinuo, Nundadaan ume he'a?" the spirit priest asks.

"Nundadaan haen ume," Harinuo replies. He looks the spirit priest in the eye. He knows the Mumbaki has little love for him, but what the spirit priest thinks does not bother him.

"I am not afraid," he whispers.

The Mumbaki nods. He pours rice wine into the dreaming cone and chants a prayer. "May the gods go with you and lighten your path," he says.

Harinuo thinks of his father. Andares was a good man, but his goodness never brought wealth. Harinuo will change all that. He has made a pact with the *Nahipan*. They said to him, "bring us blood and we will bless you."

"Shall I sacrifice a carabao?" Harinuo asked.

When they heard this, they laughed.

"Ask yourself whose blood will quench our thirst," they said.

Now, he accepts the dreaming cone from the Mumbaki. "The gods favor the bold," he says. He consumes the wine in one swallow.

To the left of him, his sisters stand in a row. They do not need to speak to remind him of his duty.

Harinuo has made up his mind to take to wife a daughter of the stars. Such an alliance will raise his status in the eyes of his tribe. He will harness the spirits to his will and he will cease to be a man with no standing.

> *Says the bird Lado-Lado:*
> *Far away you shouldn't go!*
> *Mind the snares of evil spooks*
> *That are scattered in the woods.*
> *—Ambahan from Mangyan Treasures,*
> *translated by Antoon Postma*

"Oyi Ayin Adonai. Let down your hair in the waters of the Kuywan river. Dry it in the light of the setting sun, twine it around your head like a corona, scent it with the blossoms of wild frangipani.

Daughter of the star travellers, dancer in the meadows of Yugyugan, what do you seek?"

"I am following the light of stars, my mother. I am tracing the paths they make in the deep of night. I catch their strands in my weaving tool and create patterns to confuse everyone but the wisest of the wise or the most foolish of fools."

"Darling child whose breath can calm the worst of storms, whose eyes hold light brighter than the other stars in the universe, you have walked through portals youngest ones should not walk. Headstrong and brave, wise and yet foolish. Oh young one, you do not know yet the meaning of grief. You only understand this walking under the stars, this catching of strands in your weaving tool, this tracing of new dreams and pathways. Be careful, Oyi."

"I will be careful, oh my mother. You must not weep over

me. Is it not so that all who walk among the stars hold their future within the hollow of their hands?"

"Maybe so, maybe so. But do not grow enamored of those foreign shores. There are riverbanks aplenty where your father's kingdom lies. Here, the holy grooves know you as you know them."

"I am no longer a child, oh mother. I pass through the portal. I see this world my father saw before me. I sing to these trees the melodies I learned from their brethren."

"Be careful, Oyi. Come home safe and come home soon. This mother's heart will know no rest until she knows you are home again."

Harinuo Nawotwot. Dream on under the light of stars. Wander the paths of Mount Agdanan. Tread the banks of the river Kuywan. Your fellow tribesmen have walked this way before you. Here is where the *Damuong* came up from the lowlands—they with their skins of white, their eyes the color of sky, their tongues clumsy and thick in their mouths—here, is where your brethren triumphed over them.

Pass under where their heads hang rotting from the branches of the trees. Where the ancients perform *daniw*, and speak with the spirits of the forefathers.

Harinuo passes on. He does not fear these unpopulated bones. Whose spirit speaks through the dreaming cone? Whose voice directs his footsteps?

"Up ahead," the voice says. "Up ahead is the river. There, you may rest. There you will meet your destiny."

Night has come, but Oyi is not afraid. The Karangyan trees are her friends. She has taught them the songs of the holy groves, and in turn they offer her honey from the hives of the angel bees.

Her skin glows like polished kamagong. Her hair is blue fire against the black. Her voice rings out, and swarms of fireflies gather round to warm her and to light her path.

"Little friends," Oyi says. "Thank you for the kindness of your warmth and of your light."

Harinuo dreams. He hears a goddess singing. Her voice is a summons.

"Wake up, Harinuo. Your star bride, your dream is passing by. If you are wise and good, you will ask her blessing, you will bow down and pay your respects, and when she has blessed you, you will let her go."

Night fades. Oyi still hears the refrains of songs echoing through the grove. She waves to her siblings as they travel beyond her sight to the other side.

"Go home, Oyi," her sisters sing to her.

"Let me linger another night, dear sisters," Oyi says. "Tomorrow, I willingly return to our father's groves."

"Come home, daughter," her mother sighs.

But the night is gone, and Oyi falls asleep.

> *You my darling sweet and fair*
> *Please do come along with me,*
> *To the house that's over there*
> *Everything we have is nice*
> *Whether it be plant or tree.*
> *—Ambahan from Mangyan Treasures,*
> *translated by Antoon Postma*

Morning. Harinuo awakes.

I was dreaming, Harinuo thinks. I saw a star woman walking through the trees, and father said I should let her go. As in life, he only speaks nonsense.

"I am here," he says aloud. "I am Harinuo and I will be Kadangyan."

Sweet dew drips down onto his head, and when he looks up, he sees the hive and the bees buzzing about. More honey drips down and he cups his hands. Surely the gods smile down on him today, he thinks.

When he has had his fill of honey, he goes down to the river. He sings a song as he bathes. He drinks thirstily of the cool water, and pretends he is a frog jumping about in the shallows. When he has wrung his loincloth clean, he stretches out on the rocks to dry himself.

He is almost asleep when he hears a sound.

It is the song that wakes her. Her eyes fly open and she wonders what beast could make such a lowing sound, what creature could be so wounded that it should raise its voice to disturb the harmony of nature.

In daylight, her skin retains the warm color of earth. Her long hair gleams in the sunlight, and her voice is a soft whisper.

"What could it be?" she asks the bees. But they do not reply. They go on about their business of making honey and building more hives.

Shaking off sleep, she rises from her bed of grass and scented flowers.

"Stay," the trees whisper. "Do not go."

But daylight has dissipated their memory of the language of stars, and their voices sound like rustling leaves.

Down Oyi goes, down to the riverbank, and there in the light of day, she sees a man.

He is slender like a bamboo, and yet his arms are wiry and corded with strength. In sleep, his face is peaceful.

Like and yet unlike, Oyi thinks as she draws near. *No one ever told me there was such beauty here.*

Oyi Ayin Adonai. We will sing your song ages long. Beloved of our father, darling of our mother, where have you gone? We sought for you by the banks of the Kuywan. We searched the groves of the Karangyan. We asked the bees, we sang our questions to the trees, but they could not tell us where you were.

Our mother's heart is breaking, Oyi. We will open each portal, and cross each gate until we find you, and bring you home again.

"Come," Harinuo says. He has regained his senses from seeing her the first time. "I will take you to my sisters. You are not as I expected a star woman to be, but you will suffice."

He laughs when she opens her mouth. There it is again, that string of nonsensical sounds. Like a bird chirping or a grasshopper rubbing its wings. He almost changes his mind about taking her home with him.

But when she walks back to the trees, he chases her and catches her hand in his.

"You are mine now," he says. "I will not let you go so easily."

Rough is the road over the mountains, and he clicks his teeth when her feet begin to bleed.

At first, she followed, but when she pulled her hand from his, he tied her to him with a rope that hurt her wrist and chaffed it raw.

"Let me go," she pleads. "My mother will be worried."

But he only laughs.

"Where are you taking me?" she asks.

But there is no reply.

Mother, father, sisters, brothers. All across the galaxies. The sound of their voices resonate where nighttime is.

"Oyi," they call. But Oyi walks strange paths on this side of the mountain where the people of the stars have never been.

Through the beating of the drums, through the flashing feet of dancers, through the festivity of drink and offering, Harinuo does not waver from Oyi's side.

"How strange that he should love her," the women say. And their eyes sparkle as they observe this swarthy hunter.

"I do not understand what he sees in her," they whisper to one another. "Her cheeks are like apples, and her hands are too soft."

"She is the daughter of the stars. See the marks on her forehead, behold the drawings on her palms. Her father is one of the *maknongan*."

"But how could a nawotwot win himself a daughter of a god?"

"It's not for us to question. Just look, he has done it and now you can be sure he will not remain a no-name for long."

So the conversations go.

All throughout the bride remains silent. Her eyes scan the starless sky, her hands struggle in vain against the cords of woven rattan. Her pleas for help fall on deaf ears as the drums pick up their rhythm. When ritual blood has been offered, when the spirit priest blesses the marriage bed, no one stops to think that her twittering is the voice of her protest.

At night, he imprisons her within the four walls of their hut. His hands are hot and heavy on her body; his voice is a bellow in her ear.

"Mine," he says.

When he possesses her, she remembers the warnings of her sisters and she weeps because she is not strong enough to fight him. She weeps because this place seems so far from the portal to her mother's house.

In the village, the women shun her. They turn their eyes away, and whisper to one another when she passes by. She tries to speak to them.

"Please," she says. "All I want is to go home."

But they laugh behind their hands, and turn away.

Walking through the fields, she looks for signs of her brethren, but the leaves and the stones do not sing to her of visitors from the stars.

She learns the bitterness of being a stranger unloved, and slowly she forgets the music that made her dance among the sacred trees.

"Maybe it was just a dream," she thinks. And she sinks into a mist of forgetfulness.

When her first child is born, she hears the spooks whispering together underground.

"Soon," they say to each other.

She wants to pick up her firstborn and flee, but her hands are too weak, and she cannot keep the man from taking her child. When her son's blood is spilled, she covers her ears so she will not hear the keening of the spooks underground.

"The nahipan are pleased," her husband whispers. "Now I will be Kadangyan."

> *Know the bird tigba-ungan?*
> *Once he went to Calapan,*
> *And the woods of Sablayan.*
> *There he said he changed his name*
> *But his name, oh, what a shame*
> *Tigba-ungan all the same!*
> *—Ambahan from Mangyan Treasures,*
> *translated by Antoon Postma*

Men praise him now. He has become *ya nan nunahipan*, and does what the spooks command him to do. In the first year after his marriage, the nahipan give him treasure enough to buy up rice fields and granaries belonging to the rest of the tribe. Soon, he brings the *Damuong* to his village. It is he who closes a pact with them.

"Choose," he says. And he extends his arms to encompass the places where terraces clamber up towards the skies.

Slowly, the land is parcelled up, and he marries off his sisters to the white-skinned ones.

"You mock our ways," the old chief says.

But he does not listen. He is Kadangyan now. More powerful, more wealthy than any who have gone before him. The alliances he makes fill his pockets. He enlarges his house, and builds greater granaries. He gives his captive star bride a room filled with tapestries of the night sky.

"Try to understand," he says. "If I had not offered up the child, the spooks would have taken me instead."

She does not speak, and he feels a pang of remorse remembering the smallness of his son's body.

"If you want, I can give you another child," he says.

"Seven years," the Mumbaki says when he comes to visit. "Seven years and the nahipan yearn for fresh blood."

"What do you want me to do, old man?" Harinuo asks.

"It is your choice," the Mumbaki replies.

From his window, Harinuo can look out onto terraces of rice that he now owns. His brethren harvest the rice and bind it. They pound the rice and sift it, and when it has been poured into bags, it is shipped to far-away provinces where his rice is praised as being the very best.

"What if I refuse?" he asks.

"As easily as they give, so easily they take," the old man says.

He hears the contempt in the Mumbaki's voice, and he feels that he is *nawotwot* again. Stripped of his name, he is a small man in bare feet, not worth very much at all.

"I am Kadangyan," he says to the Mumbaki. "Remember that, old man. I am Kadangyan, and I am master here."

He hits her.

She licks at the blood on her upper lip, remembering the sound the spooks made at the spilling of her firstborn's blood.

After he leaves, she looks around, and sees how she has surrendered her struggle for freedom in this cage of misery.

In her womb, she feels the first signs of quickening. She cannot go back to where she began, but she can choose to end this now. She will not let him take this child's life. She will not lose another son to the hunger of the spooks.

Outside, the stars are singing.

"Oyi," they sing. "Oyi Ayin Adonai. We sing your song. We are searching still. You are not forgotten little one."

Tears roll down her cheeks. She remembers dancing among the trees on the banks of the Kuywan. She remembers echoing back the songs of her brothers and her sisters. She remembers her mother's summons across the portal.

Starlight illuminates the rice terraces. There, her sisters are dancing among the stalks of rice. From where she sits, she hears their voices calling.

"Oyi," they call.

"Ayin," they summon.

She rises up from where she was sitting, and raising her voice she answers.

"Here," she sings. "Here, I am."

"Here?"

Whose voice was that in the darkness? Whose face looms up out of shadow? Who is it who summons him from his sleep? Who tells him of his star bride's imminent escape?

"You are mine," he says.

"No," she says. "I am my own."

"If you ask it," he says, "I will build you a larger house. I will give you richer rooms. I will buy you jewels, anything you want."

"But I never asked for any of these," she replies.

"If you go, the nahipan will take me," he cries.

"As you took me," she replies. "As you took my eldest child."

He grovels at her feet, and she remembers how enamored she was when she saw him sleeping beside the river.

"Have mercy," he pleads.

"Mercy?" she asks. "And what mercy have you shown me? What mercy will you show my second born?"

She knows the answer when he doesn't reply.

Oyi Ayin Adonai. Beautiful are you. Lost, now found, and found forevermore, dear sister.

A draft sweeps in through the open door bringing with it the scent of cosmic breezes. Warmth floods through her, and she laughs as remembrance brings back, worlds and worlds, and stars and stars, journeys and adventures she'd forgotten all about.

Her skin takes fire as it reflects the light from a million distant suns, and the weariness of earthbound flesh falls away.

"Goodbye," she cries. And her voice joins the cacophony of sound, the noise and jubilation from her former life.

The portal opens, and she steps forward. Darkness of space embraces her. Her body flows through the woodwork, breaking through the barrier of what is.

"Come back," he cried. "You are mine. Come back."

Harinuo. Eldest born of Andares. Did your father never tell you not to pluck the fruit that was not yours? Did your mother never teach you to honor the daughters of the stars?

Harinuo. Now the darkness falls, and Harinuo knows fear as he hears the gnashing of a hundred thousand tiny teeth.

ᜇᜇᜈ᜔ᜑᜌᜈ᜔ ᜑ ᜐᜓᜄᜌ᜔

DADANHAYAN HA SUGAY

The Last Full Show

Budjette Tan

Budjette Tan is the writer and co-creator of the graphic novel "Trese." By day, he writes advertising copy for McCann Worldgroup. By night (or when his boss isn't looking), he writes comic book stories. He is one of the founding members of Alamat Comics.

Initially an independently published series of photocopied comics, the Trese series has gone on to win the Philippines' National Book Award. Its heroine, Alexandra Trese, has become one of the most popular Philippine comic book characters in recent memory, a no-nonsense heroine who stands apart from many of her peers in the urban fantasy genre. This story is a rare glimpse of the softer side of Trese.

Spencer Hontiveros liked the silence of the dead better than the chatter of the living, even if the dead didn't always remain silent around him.

He had worked in the Manila City Morgue ever since he graduated from college. His father, the heart surgeon, had high hopes that he'd follow in those footsteps, or become a brain surgeon like his mother—but once Spencer had been assigned to morgue duty during med school, he knew he'd finally found his true calling.

There were times when ghosts, still bound to their cadavers, would try to send Spencer a message, but he'd learned to ignore them. He knew that he wouldn't have to deal with them after they'd been removed from his morgue.

Every now and then, however, there were ghosts who wouldn't take no for an answer, the kind who were victims of foul play and wouldn't take the injustice of it all lying down, even if their corpses were already stretched across his table. As the morgue's chief medical examiner, Spencer had seen his fair share of victims, men and women done in by gun shot, stabbing, decapitation, and speeding 18-wheeler trucks.

The worst ghosts, however, were those killed by forces that even in death they could not understand. Those were the nights when he saw bodies drained of blood and with just a hint of a puncture mark at the bellybutton; or women who'd died because of a miscarriage, but where the fetus was nowhere to be found. Those were the ghosts who simply didn't understand that there wasn't a lot that a medical examiner could do with clues that didn't come from the body itself.

Lucky for them, he knew someone who wasn't bound by the same rules, and who specialized in both crime and the supernatural. On those nights, Spencer would pick up his Nokia, hit the "8" key, and ring the first name listed under the letter "T".

"Come in, Trese!"

A lady dressed in a long black coat pushed the door open and stood by the doorway for a moment. There was something that drew the eye to her, and it was more than the way the short black hair that framed her face made it appear that she had horns. She wasn't tall, wasn't physically imposing, but she carried herself with a dangerous grace that caused many a large man to check furtively for the nearest exits. Serious, unblinking eyes surveyed the room as she walked towards Spencer, who was in the midst of filing his latest batch of reports.

"Good evening, Spunky," said Alexandra Trese, and Spencer shook his head. An old nickname from med school, one which he had never quite managed to get rid of.

"Alexandra," Spencer nodded, then looked behind her. "The boys not with you today?"

"They're on a double date." Trese glanced at the clock on the wall. "Sorry, I'm late. Had to deal with a tikbalang causing accidents on C5."

"Another horny colt on the loose?" Spencer smirked. "Did you banish him back to the mountains?"

"Unfortunately, my family and the tikbalang clan go a long way back." Her expression was not of the sort to invite further inquiry, so Spencer merely bent his head to his task as he waited for her to continue. "I left him to the tender mercies of his clan datu."

"You caught him?"

"Actually, I beat him in a race." Trese said, her tone casual, as if it were the sort of feat anyone was capable of.

Spencer's eyebrows rose appreciatively. "So, that means …"

"Yes, the tikbalang owes me three favors."

"Did you wish for world peace?"

"No." Trese gave him an inscrutable look, then switched her attention back to the clock. "So, why did you call me?"

Spencer stood between two metal gurneys and pointed to the bodies covered by a thin white sheet. "Let me introduce you to tonight's guests, Mr. and Mrs. Villaroman. Sixty Four and sixty six years old, respectively."

"Cause of death?" Trese asked.

"Heart attack."

"Natural causes?"

"From the looks of it." Spencer cleared his throat.

Trese tilted her head and stared at Spencer and he knew it was the "So-why-I-am-I-here" look. Spencer flipped open two folders from the top of the stack and started to read from two different reports.

"Location: Cinema Four on Level Four of the Robertson Mall, Ortigas."

Trese's brows furrowed as she scanned the file, and Spencer knew he finally had Trese's attention. "So, you think this has something to do with snakeboy? The one who lives in the basement of the mall?"

"He's not a snake. He's a dragon. And I already took care of him." Her tone was absentminded, her concentration clearly elsewhere. "Besides, young girls were more his thing, not grandparents."

Spencer retrieved another set of folders. "Interested yet?"

"Getting there."

"Well, maybe these will get you all in." Spencer fanned the folders on the desk like a deck of cards. "Take a look at these reports. I would've noticed them sooner but I was away on vacation."

But Trese was looking at him and not the reports. "You actually went on a vacation?" She raised an eyebrow.

"Of a sort. It was medical examiner's convention in Vegas." Spencer paused. "Honestly, I think the best part was getting dear old dad to pay for my trip. I think he was just happy that I was actually going to mingle with the living."

"The dead have their charms," Trese said, and Spencer grunted in agreement.

"And the dead have their mysteries." Spencer flipped open the files. "Here are five other deaths that have occurred in the past three months. All of the deceased were sixty years old and above. All of them died at Cinema Four in Robertson Mall at around four o'clock in the afternoon . . . And if my information is correct, I'd wager they all died at 4:44 p.m. on the dot."

Spencer glanced toward the bodies, and for just a moment, he saw an ethereal shape rise from the corpse of Mr. Villaroman, nodding its head and tapping its wrist.

Trese eyed the ghost, but didn't address it. "And all of them died of natural causes?"

"As far as I can tell. No toxins in the body. No poisons. I can think of several toxins that can make a death look like a heart attack, but the timing . . ."

Trese's eyes narrowed. "Interesting," she muttered under her breath. "Thanks Spunky."

"Long as it gets me some peace and quiet," the examiner said. "What are you going to do now?"

Trese pulled open the door, then threw a look over her shoulder. "I thought I'd catch a movie."

The afternoon crowd shambled past Trese, as she looked over their heads at the monitor displaying the schedule of Cinema Four. There was a 2:55 p.m. screening, which ended at 4:44 p.m.

Trese eased herself into the ticket line, directly behind an old married couple who still managed to radiate youthful infatuation. The wife rummaged through her purse and slowly fished out their senior citizen's cards, which granted them free admission to the movie.

The ticket seller, a pale skinned man with a bland face, smiled and asked, "Are you here for the last full show?"

The old couple tilted their heads, as if they weren't sure what they'd just been asked, but after a moment they nodded and said yes. Like many of their fellow senior citizens, the couple had become accustomed to words pitched too low for them to hear, and youngsters who would treat a request to repeat those words with impatience rather than respect. The machine spat out two tickets, and the old couple strolled toward the cinema as Trese stepped up to the counter.

The ticker seller looked at her, smiled, and said, "Ticket for one?" Trese waited for the seller to ask her about the last full show, but the man only stared at Trese expectantly. After a long minute, Trese answered in the affirmative, took her ticket, and headed for Cinema Four.

Inside, Trese saw an old man seated at the front row. He was laughing so hard he was in tears. There were three grannies in the middle section who giggled like school girls.

She spotted the old couple that entered before her. They were holding hands. The wife was sobbing, yet smiling. Her husband leaned over, wiped away her tears and whispered, "This is my favorite part."

Trese's gaze lingered on the light coming from the projector booth then followed it to the wide, white screen—which showed nothing.

With a wary deliberation, Trese made her way to a locked door marked RESTRICTED AREA. From the confines of her coat, she pulled out a dagger –a kris—that seemed to emit a faint glow that pushed back the darkness ever so slightly. She placed the tip of the blade on the doorknob, tapped it three times and whispered, "*Bukas*".

The door unlocked itself and obediently opened for Trese.

Up the stairs to the projection room, she found another pale skinned man keeping watch over the movie projector. She quickly noticed the markings on the projector. Painted on machine that spun and whirred were sigils required for spellcasting. A summoning spell.

"Who are you?" Trese pointed at the man with her kriss. "What are you showing these people?"

"Ms. Trese!" The pale man turned to her with an expression

of happy surprise. It was not a look that Trese was accustomed to seeing. "My associate told me you were here! Call me Ishmael. My associate outside is Lino. I apologize for not informing you we already set up shop in the city. Our Mistress Sidapa told us to get your permission first."

Sidapa, Trese thought. An entity best dealt with at arms length, and with a healthy amount of caution. Trese considered this, and decided against running him through. Instead, she pushed Ishmael against the wall and leaned the blade of her kris against his neck.

"You didn't answer my second question," Trese said.

"You dare?" The pale man's eyes were wide with indignation. "I serve the—"

"—Goddess of Death of the North. I know." Trese pushed the blade harder against his skin, even as she kept her voice level. "That still doesn't tell me what you're doing in my city."

Ishmael looked down his nose at Trese's blade, and his mouth curled up in a sneer. "You think a servant of Sidapa is afraid of death?"

"I wouldn't kill you, Ishmael," she answered. "Not for a while."

A small smiled flickered across her face, then was gone. So was Ishmael's sneer.

"We—we just thought this would be easier, rather than waiting for all these people to die, then scrambling across Luzon, picking up their souls." He held up his hands quickly. "It's not just convenience! We provide a service. We let them review their lives one last time—that's what they see on the screen. After, they decide if they still have any unfinished business. If they decide that all is well, we let them doze off, before we punch their ticket."

Trese dragged him to the side until she had a clear view of the theater below. She looked down at the people reliving their lives, at the emotions vivid on their face. To face death knowingly, unsurprised, the details of your life fresh in your mind . . . Trese wondered if that was how she would go, if the choice were given to her.

The thought was gone as soon as it arrived. Warrior and healer, child of paradox and possibility . . . she would die as she had lived.

With her free hand, Trese pulled out her cellphone. "Spunky, I think you'll be seeing more guests coming from Cinema Four. I want you to give me an update every time one comes in, especially if they deviate from the usual pattern."

Trese pocketed the phone, then released her grip on Ishmael, and returned her kris beneath her jacket. "If you're conning these people to give up their souls, if you're running some sort of *kaluluwa* smuggling operation, believe me when I tell you that not even Sidapa will be able to protect you from me."

Ishmael looked down and nodded his head. "Yes, ma'am."

She was about to step out of the booth when Ishmael said, "Perhaps I can offer you something Ms. Trese, to make up for any breach of protocol, on behalf of myself and my compatriot."

Trese turned back to him, but said nothing.

Ishmael held up a ticket. "Is there anything you'd like to see?"

Trese picked a seat near the exit. On the screen, she watched her younger self celebrate her eighth birthday. Trese stayed just long enough to see her mom read her a bedtime story, and then she stood and left the theater.

She knew how that particular night would end. It was the reason she had bound herself to protect the city from the forces of the underworld, the reason why she wouldn't die in a quiet theater with a full heart and a smile on her face. She would die with a blade in her hand. She would die doing her job, her duty. Trese knew that.

But, for a few precious moments, it had been good to remember a time when she'd believed otherwise.

DAGAU

The Alipin's Tale

Raymond G. Falgui

Raymond G. Falgui teaches at the University of the Philippines. His short stories have appeared in the Philippines Free Press, Philippines Graphic, and Playboy Philippines magazines, as well as the Likhaan, Philippine Speculative Fiction, and Digest of Philippine Genre Stories anthologies. His articles on gaming have appeared in Azagar's Book of Rituals and The Kobold Quarterly. He is also a self-proclaimed Luddite who last owned a cell phone some time in 2004.

Lapu-Lapu is the first "historical" Philippine hero, a chieftain who rejected and repelled a European force led by Ferdinand Magellan. While textual accounts of the "Battle of Mactan" survive, many of the details—including the extent of Lapu-Lapu's actual participation in the battle—have been lost to history. The battle itself has been elevated to the level of myth. But what would happen if we took things one step further?

The *datus* and rajahs have forbidden that this tale be told, have proclaimed that death shall come to the teller of this tale. Listen carefully while I whisper it.

Listen: You know the tale of how the great Lapu-Lapu saved our world from the *Kastila*, the men with skin paler than the flesh of any milkfish. On the day of that great battle, the waters around Mactan turned red with *Kastila* blood (for though their skin was of a different color, their blood was red like ours). On that day, the *datus* and rajahs gave thanks to the *bathalas*, for the *Kastila* were driven back to their ships and our world was restored to the way it had always been.

The usurper and upstart Humabon was soon dealt with. Without his *Kastila* friends, he was helpless when the *datus* and rajahs returned to reclaim Cebu. The magic statue the *Kastila* priest gave him lost its power,[1] and Humabon and his wife fled on a *bangka* into the open sea, where a wave swallowed them. For the *bathalas* were angry with Humabon for his apostasy, for turning his face away from them to worship the *bathala* of the *Kastila*.

This tale or parts of it you already know, but do you know the rest? Do you know that less than a full moon after that glorious day, Lapu-Lapu did what no *Kastila* could do, and destroyed our world forever?

I know this for I was there, for was I not Lapu-Lapu's faithful *alipin*, loyal and dependable and always at his master's side? I was there beside him on the day of the battle. But even more important, I was there by his side on the night *before* the battle.

That was when we kept watch for the arrival of the *bathalas*.

The arrival of the *Kastila* had shaken the *datus* and rajahs. The ease with which the *Kastila* had defeated the rightful rajah of Cebu, and placed Humabon in his place, terrified them. Ever since the forgotten time when our people first took these islands from the small, dark folk of the mountains, the *datus* and rajahs had made a compact with the *bathalas* of the land.

---

[1] This is a reference to the Sto. Nino of Cebu, which is reputed to have miraculous powers. This relic is believed to be the same one that Magellan gave to Humabon and his wife. It was lost after Magellan's defeat, but was rediscovered after the Spaniards returned to Cebu in 1565.

In return for the worship of our people, the *bathalas* promised the *datus* and rajahs that they and their descendants would rule for all time. Thus it had been, until Humabon.

I have heard it said that Humabon was a man of small repute, a farmer whose crops were barely enough to provide sufficient tribute to the rajah of Cebu. I have heard it said that Humabon was not even this, that he was an *alipin* of the rajah who saw his chance when the *Kastila* slew his master. Whatever the truth, the *Kastila* raised up Humabon as the new rajah of Cebu.

The compact had been broken. The rule of the *datus* and rajahs was no longer forever. Perhaps, some whispered, the new *bathala* of the *Kastila* was stronger than the *bathalas* of the land.

To silence this talk, the *bathalas* commanded Lapu-Lapu to ready his warriors for battle. The *Kastila* were coming to Mactan, the *bathalas* said, and Lapu-Lapu would defeat them.

In his fear, Lapu-Lapu hid his face in the dirt.

"How can I fight the *Kastila*?" Lapu-Lapu asked the earth. "They carry their *bathala* with them. I shall be killed like the rajah of Cebu, and some nameless *alipin* shall rule in my place."

"Be not afraid," the *bathalas* said. "We shall strike at the *Kastila* on the night before the battle. We shall bleed and weaken them. You and your warriors shall strike the death blow."

At these pleasing words Lapu-Lapu lifted his dirt-streaked face and gave praise to the *bathalas*. He ordered that crops and pigs be burned and sacrificed to them.

But on the night before the battle, Lapu-Lapu stood watch over the small encampment the *Kastila* had built beside their ships. He wished to make certain the *bathalas* would keep their promise.

He was no fool, my master, but he did not fear enough.

He feared the *bathalas*, whether those of the land or the *Kastila*, and he feared his fellow *datus* and rajahs, but nothing else.

Even after the rise of Humabon, he saw no danger in bringing an *alipin* along with him.

In the darkest hours of the night, the *Kastila* were visited by the spirits of the land. But it was not the man-spirits, the *bathalas* with their voices like thunder, who appeared. Instead, it was the woman-spirits of the land, the *diwatas* with their sweet voices and soft laughter, who brought doom down upon the *Kastila*.

The *diwatas* moved fearlessly among the *Kastila*, both those asleep and those awake. They feared no weapon, for no weapon would be raised against them except one, and that one the *diwatas* wielded absolute power over. Their brown skin held an endless fascination for the pale *Kastila*, whose eyes grew wide in their heads. These eyes followed the motion of the *diwatas'* naked bodies, swaying side to side with the gyrations of those well-rounded hips, moving up and down with the rise and fall of those mountainous breasts. The *Kastila* who were awake fell to their knees and embraced the *diwatas'* knees, sobbing with gratefulness. The sleeping *Kastila* raised their arms, and laughing *diwatas* fell atop them, making their dreams into reality.

I laughed aloud, for I realized the *diwatas'* plan. After a night of supernatural pleasure, the *Kastila* would be weak and spent come the dawn. My master and his warriors would slaughter them like pigs.

The sound of my laughter attracted the attention of one of the *diwatas*, who turned to look at us.

My master had turned to strike me for giving our position away, but the *diwata's* eyes held him. Against his will, he stared at her. Smiling, she began to dance.

Soon my master lost all thought of punishing me. Then he lost all thought altogether.

I was grateful to the *diwata* for her intervention. She had saved me from what would have been a painful beating—my master has little patience for the mistakes of an *alipin*.

But I wondered at her actions, for before my own eyes were captured by the *diwata's* dance, before my own thoughts flew away from me as I watched the movements of her breasts and hips, I understood two things:

One, this *diwata*, whose countenance shone so bright even amidst so much beauty, could be none other than Maria Makiling, the greatest of the *diwatas*, the mountain goddess from the great island of Luzon to the north.

Two, it was not for Lapu-Lapu that she was dancing; it was for me.

Seven days after the great battle of Mactan, my master lay close to death. Lapu-Lapu had defeated the *Kastila*, but another enemy had conquered him.

He lay on his mat and shook, his body burning, but he did not have the blood fever that often comes from battle wounds. No weapon of the *Kastila* had touched him; he had led his warriors and killed nine of the enemy himself in the battle—if one could call it that. One *Kastila* had worn such a dreamy, happy expression on his dead face that his head had been thrown away instead of being made into a trophy.

"Eat some rice gruel, my master," I said.

He slapped the wooden bowl from my hand.

"I hunger for only one thing," he answered. He turned his head towards the wall and moaned like a wounded beast.

It was clear to all that he would soon die unless something was done. Thus, none thought it suspicious when I voiced my suggestion, desperate as they were to save my master's life.

"On the night of the coming full moon, the *bathalas* will hold a feast to celebrate the defeat of the *Kastila*," I told Lapu-Lapu.

"I know where the feast shall be held. I shall lead you there, my master. Ask the *bathalas* a reward for defeating the *Kastila*.

"Ask them to let you have your way with Maria Makiling."

Upon hearing my words, Lapu-Lapu recovered at once and took food for the first time in days. My master saw the wisdom in my words, for while the *bathalas* were above the *datus* and rajahs, the *diwatas*—like all women—were beneath them.

If a *diwata* could be caught or commanded, she would belong to the *datu* who had conquered her.

"Let us leave now," Lapu-Lapu said, shoveling rice into his mouth with his fingers. He ate ravenously, but took no pleasure from his food.

"The full moon is still many days away," I said. "And there is much we must do if we are to invite ourselves to the *bathalas'* feast."

At my advice, my master sent his servants to the forest to cut down all the bamboo trees they could find. In the meantime, my master slaked his lust on his wives and servant girls, though his desire for Maria Makiling still caused his body to shake.

When all was ready, my master and I left for our journey. We did not have far to travel: the *bathalas* and *diwatas* did not live in our world, but there are many places in our world that touch their land, and finding these places is not hard. The difficulty is that no one passes into the world of the *bathalas* without getting past the guardian—the last of the giant race, the *higante* Bernardo Carpio.

It would take a cunning trick to get past such a fearful guardian, but I had prepared my master well

"Bernardo Carpio," he shouted to the giant. "I am Lapu-Lapu, *datu* of Mactan and victor over the pale *Kastila*. It is because of my brave deeds that the *bathalas* feast on this day. It is only fitting that I should be allowed to join them."

The giant shook its head.

"I see the justice of your claim, Lapu-Lapu, but neither *bathalas* nor *datus* are known for their justice. My masters shall beat me harshly if I grant you entrance."

"Then let us share a drink before I go, that we may part as friends. Let me drink your rice wine and I shall let you drink mine—the finest rice wine produced by my people."

Bernardo Carpio readily agreed, for the *bathalas* always left him the worst rice wine for his drink. He longed to taste the fine rice wine enjoyed by the *datus* and rajahs. He exchanged his giant bamboo container with Lapu-Lapu's much smaller one, and both giant and *datu* began to drink.

I let them drink for half the night, before I roused my master to his feet. Bernardo Carpio's rice wine was of a foul taste and even fouler smell, but there was much of it—too much for my poor master, who now staggered as he walked and would have fallen if not for my support. He did not even notice the gift I slipped around his neck.

As for Bernardo Carpio, he continued to drink from Lapu-Lapu's bamboo container, little realizing that the end of it was attached to another bamboo pole, then another, and another, stretching all the way to the sea. Bernardo Carpio was trying to drink the sea—an impossible task—but so great was his desire for fine rice wine that he refused to stop.

Making our way past the preoccupied giant, my master

and I arrived at last at the great feast. As planned, the feast was nearing its end when our arrival was announced. By that time the *bathalas* had feasted much, and were in an indulgent enough mood to listen to Lapu-Lapu's petition.

"My masters," I said, "I speak for Lapu-Lapu, the great *datu* of Mactan who stands and staggers behind me."

The appreciative laughter of the *bathalas* greeted my words.

"He struck the killing blow against the *Kastila*, and now asks a boon of you."

"What does your master want?" asked one of the *bathalas*.

Before I could continue, my master gave voice to his desire.

"Maria Makiliiiiing," he crooned—the song of every drunken lover.

"Maria Makiliiiiing," he cried, like a dog howling at the moon.

There was some laughter from the more inebriated *bathalas*, but the rest frowned.

"Not for killing a hundred *Kastila* will we let you take Maria Makiling from us," said the *bathala* who had spoken earlier.

"Not for a thousand!"

"My masters," I pleaded, "Lapu-Lapu does not wish to take Maria Makiling away from you. He only wishes to have his way with her. Then his lust for her will be spent, and he will be able to live out his life in peace."

At this explanation the *bathalas* were placated.

"Ah, that's different," said the first *bathala*. "Of course we will grant such a reasonable request."

Many of the *bathalas* clapped their hands at the thought of the upcoming entertainment.

"Call Maria Makiling!" they shouted. "We shall have some fine sport at the end of our feast."

But the *diwatas* bowed their heads and withdrew from the

feast out of shame for their sister.

The *bathalas* formed a loud, lusty circle, and Maria Makiling appeared in the middle of it. I felt a rage fill my heart at the thought of her violation, but Maria Makiling read my heart and looked at me. In her eyes, I saw a warning: not yet.

Lapu-Lapu staggered into the circle, cheered on by the *bathalas*. He found himself before Maria Makiling, who shed her garments and lay down on the grass before him. She spread her legs, her breasts rising and falling with each breath.

Lapu-Lapu stared down at this vision of beauty. He lowered his loincloth and prepared to take her.

Nothing happened. Lapu-Lapu had drunk too much wine.

While Lapu-Lapu looked down at himself in sadness and chagrin, the *bathalas* started to laugh. The sight of the disappointed *datu* was too much for even the most sober *bathalas*; forgetful of their guest's shame, they joined in the laughter and merriment. Soon, many of the *bathalas* were laughing so hard that they rolled around on the ground, helpless and blind to their danger.

For the madness of wine and humiliation had overwhelmed Lapu-Lapu's senses. He drew his kris even as he pulled up his undergarments, and without thought or premeditation he struck one of the prone *bathalas* a killing blow.

Such a rash act should have been his doom, for no man—not even a *datu* or a rajah—can strike at a *bathala* and live.

But Lapu-Lapu did not die.

Instead, he and the other *bathalas* looked on in dazed wonder as the *kris* sliced off the prone *bathala's* head. The head fell to the ground and rolled to Lapu-Lapu's feet, a look of surprise and wonderment still upon it.

A new madness came into Lapu-Lapu at that moment; a fresh lust brightened his eyes. Driven by this new desire, Lapu-Lapu attacked the *bathalas*.

Some tried to fight him, but the fire and lightning they called forth would not even touch the *datu*. In contrast, it seemed that every scratch or cut inflicted by the *datu's* blade turned into a fatal wound. One *bathala* screamed in agony as the slight gash on his elbow filled with a white flame that consumed first his arm, then the rest of him.

Others called on Bernardo Carpio to save them, but the giant was unable to move, his stomach heavy from trying to drink up the sea. With their dying breaths, the *bathalas* cursed him bitterly.[2]

As Lapu-Lapu continued to kill, I grabbed Maria Makiling by the hand and together we fled that place of slaughter.

At dawn, we came out of our hiding place to find all the *bathalas* dead. My former master lay amongst them, covered in blood but unhurt.

I went to Lapu-Lapu and removed the talisman I had slipped on his neck after we left Bernardo Carpio. It was a strange thing, this talisman made of silver: at the end of its chain was a small cross similar to the large wooden one the *Kastila* had carried. I had taken the talisman from one of the

---

[2] The myth of Bernardo Carpio is tied to the earthquakes he creates as he attempts to escape his prison. According to some versions of the myth, he was imprisoned to stop him from leading the Filipinos in rebellion against the Spaniards (http://www.katig.com/alamat02.html). In Nick Joaquin's *Pop Stories for Groovy Kids*, he seeks to escape his chains to lead the Filipino people to a golden age of freedom and prosperity. I have altered the myth by suggesting that Bernardo Carpio deserves his punishment, while at the same time providing a motivation for his future actions: if he is coming back to restore Filipino freedom, perhaps he had something to do with the loss of it in the first place.

fallen *Kastila*. I did not understand its power.

But Maria Makiling understood: she had appeared to me on the night after the battle, and commanded me to retrieve it. She understood that the *bathalas* were afraid of the *bathala* of the *Kastila*, afraid that the power of this new *bathala* could hurt them, perhaps even destroy them.

So, to protect themselves, our brave *bathalas* had sent the *diwatas* to fight in their place.

Their plan worked, but it was that moment of cowardice that turned Maria Makiling against them.

"I've had enough of *bathalas* for lovers," she said then, reading my mind.

"And I'll have nothing to do with *datus* and rajahs either."

"From now on, all my lovers will be like you. Even when you are dirt, in honor of your memory I shall take only lovers who remind me of you."

Her hand caressed my cheek: "The quiet, lowly men of the earth—loyal and faithful and true."[3]

I stared in awe at the fallen *bathalas*.

"What happens now?" I asked her. "I did all that you commanded, leading Lapu-Lapu here and baiting the trap for Bernardo Carpio. But what does this mean for our world?"

"It means that our world will change at last," she said. "Does that bother you?"

"Given that I am *alipin* in this world, I will not weep to see it pass away," I said.

But I could not help asking: "What will take its place?"

"The pact made by the *datus* and rajahs was with the *bathalas*, not the *diwatas*.

---

[3] This is a reference to the Maria Makiling myth wherein she chooses a lowly farmer over two more powerful and prosperous suitors (http://en.wikipedia.org/wiki/Maria_Makiling).

"My sisters and I owe no obligation to the former, and thanks to you we are now free of the latter.

"When the *Kastila* return, there will be no *bathalas* to protect the *datus* and rajahs. The *Kastila* will crush them."

"Then we will have only traded one cruel master for another," I said.

"As for the *Kastila*," Maria Makiling said, "their priests are also *datus* and rajahs, but this new *bathala*, this HesuKristo, was an *alipin* like yourself. His spirit will come to your aid against the *datus* and rajahs."

"And even if He does not, remember what has happened here.

"*Datus* and rajahs you shall always have with you," Maria Makiling said, "whether their skin be fair or brown.

"The *bathalas* are gone, but the *diwatas* remain. Call on us, and together we will make a world where *datus* and rajahs and even *bathalas* can fall."

She smiled.

"Perhaps even a world where women rule over men."

She laughed at the expression on my face, pushed me to the earth, then fell atop me.

"It will not be so bad," she said.

HALIYA

Keeper of My Sky

Timothy James Dimacali

Timothy James M. Dimacali has always been fascinated by the intersection of science and mythology. He is currently the Science and Technology Editor of GMA News Online, but loves to play his violin every now and then. He has been a fellow for fiction at the annual Silliman University National Writers Workshop and the Iligan National Writers Workshop, and graduated with a degree in Creative Writing from the University of the Philippines.

The people of Panay tell the story of the god Tungkung Langit's eternal search for his wife, the goddess Alunsina. They speak of how Tungkung Langit scattered Alunsina's jewels in the sky in an effort to call her back to him; how her necklace became the stars; her comb, the moon; her crown, the sun. According to the old story, she never returned. Perhaps she had a good reason.

The first moments of existence are always the most painful.

Tungkung Langit's consciousness was scattered across the void, little tiny flecks of awareness that danced above the surface of the spacetime stream like so many fireflies in the dark nothingness beyond the Universe.

The slivers of his awareness told him what he already knew: the Universe spread out around him in shimmering effervescent rivulets of time and space—coalescing, branching, converging, extending in all directions well beyond the farthest reach of even his own most distant avatar.

He knew this Universe well. Apart from him, there was only one other who understood it as much as himself. Their actions were the impetus for its creation, after all. It was their offspring. Their child.

And she was there, somewhere, within it. His avatars searched for her as they darted cautiously about the spacetime currents, each an entire reality unto itself.

So many worlds…

He looked for a promising current from among the near infinitude of realities that swirled about him. His avatars hovered above the branching courses of spacetime. Searching. Yearning.

Which one? This one?

He narrowed his search to a finite set of similar worlds. He summoned the fragments of his consciousness to himself, gathering them together in preparation for his descent into existence.

Perhaps. Yes.

His consciousness coalesced around the thought, a mote of hope that swelled within him and gave him the immense strength needed to collapse the wave-functions of his being into a single world-line entity that even now hurtled forward, down into his chosen course.

To exist, one must be born into pain.

He called out to the scattered fragments of his distended consciousness, and they responded from across the void. The slivers of his being came to him, each with its own song, echoes in the still vastness between realities.

As they gathered, the soft susurrus of their lonely symphonies grew in an agonizing crescendo, exploding in a cacophony of dissonant voices.

Then, silence.

Tungkung Langit opened his eyes to find himself descending into a sea of stars. They rushed up to meet him, bright blue flecks that turned hot-white then faded into crimson embers as they passed, red-shifted against the darkness of space.

He did not know how long or how far he fell. But at last, the stars gave way to a blue-black sky above a light-speckled city. Vapor condensed around him as he fell, transformed in his wake into a downpour of heavy rain.

Somewhere on the other side of the city, on a sidewalk, a man in a black jacket raises his umbrella against the downpour. He cradles in his other hand a large bouquet of roses, wrapped tightly in brown paper and plastic.

He is meeting his wife for dinner at a nearby restaurant. It is their anniversary, and he hopes to surprise her. He sees her at the window, distracted by a paperback book. Flowers in hand, he walks up to the entrance—and vanishes.

Inside the restaurant, the woman looks up from her reading. She feels, fleetingly, that she is forgetting something. She shrugs off the thought and continues to read. She is having dinner alone as usual, and waits for her order to be served.

The legends say that, when it rains, it is the god of the sky crying for his lost love. But the truth of the matter is this: in the beginning, there was no rain, nor even a universe to speak of.

There was just the both of them, two gods together in the void. They did not even have names for each other then. Names, after all, are born out of causality and separation. But in the nowhere and nowhen before all else existed, time and division had no meaning.

They made love together, hand in hand, in the darkness before existence. Each touch tingled with the potency of creation: as she took his girth into her embrace, he caressed the small of her back with his fingertips and she trembled, exhaling a sweet breath of newborn stars.

They held each other, together alone in the primordial void, whispering to each other oracles of futures yet untold.

Together, they created the universe. But it would not be a painless birth.

The physical laws that they had set into motion necessitated an internal observer, a solitary watcher who could fix the universe's initial state and ensure its stability as it expanded; it also required an outside caretaker, a custodian to watch over its unfolding.

The beginning of the universe was the end of their union, and the echo of their parting would fill the sky forever. Thenceforth, across all timestreams and all realities, the memory of that painful birth would haunt the dreams of all living things. All races would know them forevermore by the names dictated by their chosen functions: Alunsina, the Lone One, and Tungkung Langit, Keeper of the Sky.

Now, an apartment. It exists here, and in many other worlds like this one, in forms appropriate for each. Other beings in other realities see it in their own way, but here it appears as just that—a medium-sized room with white floor tiles, a not uncomfortable bed with mint green sheets, a bookshelf filled with scented candles and paperback volumes, a polished driftwood sidetable: an apartment.

Outside, the rain falls in sheets from a dark grey sky. Raindrops spatter onto the thin glass of the windowpane, where they streak down seemingly random paths to the balcony floor.

In this reality, Alunsina waits. She looks out the window, stares intently at the falling rain as it courses down the glass. She sees patterns there, telltale signs that glisten in the flash of distant lightning.

A mother tucks in her child to sleep. In the child's hands is a teddy bear, faded and worn and missing one brown button eye. The mother runs her fingers through the soft black curls of his hair and remembers his father, gone these many years.

The child, frightened by the pummeling rain and drumming thunder outside, asks his mother to tell him a story. She obliges, and begins to open her mouth when she suddenly realizes that she misses her husband and wishes that they had had at least one child before he passed away. She walks out of her bedroom, wondering what it would have been like to have a son with hair black and curled like his father's.

Alunsina looks out at the auguring rain, and knows its full portent.

"He's here," she whispers to herself, her voice as clear as crystal glass. She gets up and prepares for Tungkung Langit's arrival. She feels anticipation—and fear.

Alunsina stands in front of the bathroom mirror, cold water

flooding into the basin. She pulls back her hair and reaches down for a handful of water. She splashes it onto her face and on her neck. She breathes deeply.

It has been many billions of years since last she saw her lover. And though she had always wished for this day, she also hoped that it would never come.

She remembers the many eons she spent alone in the primordial Universe, stripped of most of her avatars and trapped in this one body, the only constant in a continually evolving Universe.

Countless ages passed before the first worlds came into existence, and much longer before the first stirrings of life came into being.

And through it all, she was there, tending to the Universe that was their child. She ached with the loneliness that only a god could know, and she knew that his pain and yearning were no less than hers.

It was only a matter of time before he found her.

In a hospital room, a priest prays over a dying grandmother during her final moments. They are surrounded by her weeping children and grandchildren.

A frail, knotted old hand reaches out to touch the priest's robes. He leans forward to hear her confession.

She whispers to him a lifetime of knowledge and wisdom and experience. Joys, pains, triumphs, regrets. She wonders if it was all worth it.

He tells her yes, it was, yes.

The priest makes the sign of the cross as the old woman expires. The room is silent, save for the sound of the rain outside. He is saddened that the old woman died alone with no one to remember her, no relatives to mourn her passing, no other witnesses to give her life meaning.

Alunsina feels the timestreams falling apart, the fabrics of reality unraveling. She is afraid, but knows what must be done.

She had kept herself hidden for so long that she had forgotten what it was like to be in his presence, to feel him close to her. Now, trembling and afraid, she closed her eyes and called out to him.

Outside, the rain stopped.

She sensed Tungkung Langit's presence, and spoke first.

"You know you're not supposed to be here."

Tungkung Langit hesitated. These were not the words he had hoped to hear.

"Are you not going to ask me why I came? Or how hard it was for me to find you?"

"I know why you're here. Just as you know why you can't stay."

"You could have stopped me from coming here. You sensed my arrival. You could have left."

"No, I couldn't. I have my responsibilities. And so do you."

Tungkung Langit acknowledged the truth of her words. Long ago, he watched her as she fell towards the nascent Universe, at the dawn of all things. He saw the determination in her eyes as she pulled away from him, the steadiness of her hands and the look of calm acceptance on her face: this is what she wanted all along.

"You were always the stronger one," he said.

Alunsina wished so much to touch his face, to hold him in her arms once again. But she couldn't—not without shifting the Universe's precarious balance, not without collapsing the timestreams together.

He yearned for completion, for wholeness. Alunsina felt it too. Even now, it was all she could do to keep the Universe from collapsing.

Tungkung Langit cleared his throat.

"I was okay for the first few millennia. I was . . . I am . . . proud of our child. And yes, I love it dearly. But I need you with me."

"I know," Alunsina nodded. "But I need you more to be the keeper of my sky."

They stood barely a hairsbreadth from each other, looking into each others' eyes, waiting for the Universe to end.

Tungkung Langit knew what he had to do.

He pulled away, stepping off into the void and back up into the cold night sky. Alunsina watched his ascent into the star-filled firmament. She saw him glow brightly even as he grew smaller and smaller until at last he vanished in the distance, transformed into a fleeting star that flickered briefly and then was gone.

At that precise moment, a chill wind passed over her. She felt the tiniest drop of water fall upon her lips. One by one the raindrops came, and yet she still looked up at the empty blackness that marked her lover's passing.

The cold rain fell into her eyes and onto her face, and she did not know if she was crying. All she knew was that, as far and as long as she could remember, it had never rained so hard.

HALUPE

Conquering Makiling

Mo Francisco

Mo Francisco climbs and writes as much as she can. Her stories have come out in the Philippines Free Press, Philippines Graphic, Speculative Fiction IV and other publications. Her story "Jimmie" won 2nd place in the Philippines Free Press Literary Awards in 2009. She has climbed with both the Loyola and the UP Mountaineers. They have taught her that going days without a shower, sleeping on rocks and suffering limatik bites are worth the trouble when you stand on top of the world with a blanket of clouds below you, music blasting from an iPod and good friends beside you, their glasses raised. She has yet to encounter Maria on her climbs.

In myths, Maria Makiling is almost the prototypical nature goddess: caring, benevolent, and always generous to men of humble origins. That generosity of spirit at times becomes an offering of her own heart, as Maria is often portrayed as taking human lovers. Yet perhaps in constructing such a romantic image of the goddess, we've left something out. This story uses a modern context to explore a more primal aspect of our most popular diwata.

I met Maria on a sultry mid-May day. It had just finished raining. It shouldn't even have rained that time of year, but, you know, climate change and all that shit. The *alimuom* smell of mud and wet asphalt was in the air. The heat rose from the ground in waves thick enough to make a statue sweat.

I was at the Makiling High School campus, touring the small cluster of cottages that served as dormitories, libraries, classrooms, and studios, depending on the needs of the students. My dad had assigned my cousin Tonton to be my tour guide in Los Baños, and I was waiting for him to get out of his summer class.

"I don't know Tito," Tonton had teased. "A day without X-box? Can the Manila boy handle it?"

With eyes still glued to the TV screen and thumbs flying over the controller, I'd replied: "Bring it on!"

So there I was, my thumbs itching for my controller, the sun beating down on me like there was no ozone layer. My sweat was staining the thin fabric of my vintage tee, making me wish that I had put on deodorant that morning. But when I saw Maria, I wished I had sprayed on Axe—you know that brand with all the commercials that show how horny girls get once they get a whiff.

She sat behind a booth with a sign I couldn't quite read. Maria wasn't beautiful, not really. I mean, no Pond's commercial would pick her as their endorser. It's not like she was acne-riddled, she didn't have any warts or anything, but she wasn't 'rosy white' either. Maria was dark-skinned—not even that 'olive-skinned' kind of dark that people describe as beautiful. Her complexion was a lusterless, uninspiring, nut-brown. But her limbs were lean with muscle, her hair a forest framing her face, and there was a wild glint in her eyes. She was hot.

As I approached, I was able to read the words written on the sign hanging on the booth.

Makiling Eco Friends: Tree Nurturing Sign-ups

She was talking to a girl who had a pen poised over the volunteer sign-up sheet. Maria was doodling while talking; her leg propped up on the seat, her sketchpad on her knee.

When I got closer, I saw that her doodle was really a charcoal portrait of the newest volunteer.

"Yes, call time is six a.m. Pack your lunch and bring water, a change of clothes and sun block."

The air was still and thick with heat. She scooped up her mass of hair, and, with a pencil, twirled it like spaghetti, using the pencil to keep the knot in place. I watched her move as if in slow motion. My eyes followed a lone bead of sweat as it traveled down the length of her newly-exposed neck, down her collarbones and into the hint of cleavage that peeked out from the low neckline of her tank top. My mouth was open as I debated whether the curve I spied was her breast or a trick of light and shadow.

"Can I help you?"

I blinked and looked at her. Her eyes were stormy and her nostrils flared. The other girl was gone. I clamped my mouth shut.

"Uh," I blurted, "I was reading what was on your shirt?"

"There's nothing written on my shirt." She pointed down at the graphic illustration. "It's a tree."

"Yeah, I meant –"

"Am I seeing you on the sixth or the seventh?"

"What?" I could feel my ears burning up.

She handed me a pen, "Which day will you be volunteering for? I think I'll sign you up for both." She looked at me. "Well? What's your name?"

"Thomas." I managed to say.

"Well Peeping Thomas, call time is six a.m. Pack your lunch and bring water, overnight clothes and sun block." She handed me a photocopy of reminders. "Look for me. Maria."

The pamphlet she gave me was a powdery photocopy that summarized the state of the Makiling Forest and stressed the need to plant more trees. According to the pamphlet, the

Makiling Forest Reserve is one of the few remaining old-growth rainforests in Luzon and illegal logging has a negative impact on the biodiversity of the area. It went on to say that the landslides in the recent years were due to erosion, noting that across Luzon, 157,000 hectares of trees are cut down every year.

The statistics smudged off onto my hand the moment I turned the page.

The only tree I was thinking about was the one on her shirt, the only hills, the ones peeking from beneath her tank top. When the word 'virgin' popped in my mind, I certainly wasn't thinking about forests.

So, yeah, I volunteered.

On Saturday I woke up early and snuck out of Tonton's room, where I was bunking until my dad finished his business in Los Baños. I didn't invite Tonton. I was supposed to be his smooth cousin from the city. The last thing I needed was to listen to him make some crack about the city boy hitting on a local girl. Maria got me tongue-tied enough without the added pressure of Tonton critiquing my every move.

At the meeting place, Maria was already waiting with a handful of other volunteers. When she saw me approaching, she thumped on the side of the stainless steel jeep and the engine sputtered to life. Everyone piled in and she gestured to me to follow her.

"Didn't think you'd come." She smiled.

I shrugged in a manner that I hoped looked nonchalant, but I admit that I was distracted by her shorts—or apparent lack thereof—which revealed long, sinewy, tan legs. I imagined positioning myself behind her for a good view as she bent down over the saplings.

"Want to be on top?" she asked.

"What?" I squeaked.

"Top load." She said and with her lips pointed to the metal rigging on top of the jeep. "There's not enough room for all of us."

I managed a nod and positioned myself under the metal ladder on the side of the jeep. "Ladies first," I said.

She laughed and shook her head. "You first. I won't have you staring at my ass on the way up." I must have looked guilty because she laughed again and pushed me forward. After scaling the side, I turned around and extended my hand.

"I got it." She said. She scaled the ladder faster than I had, and while wearing a full sixty five-liter mountaineering pack, too. She threw her pack down and arranged the other packs to create a cushion, then promptly lay down on her makeshift bed. She thumped on the roof with the palm of her hand. "Let's go, Mang Gerry!"

The jeep started with a jerk and I lost my balance, falling hard on my ass. I cursed under my breath.

"Better brace yourself Thomas. It's gonna be a bumpy ride."

As the jeep left the town and began the ascent up the mountain, the cement road became a dust road. The mountain loomed before us, a thick white mist enshrouding its slopes in mystery.

While Maria reclined comfortably on the packs, I was busy avoiding decapitation, dodging the electric wires that came hurtling toward me at fifty kilometers an hour. As I'm quite attached to my head, you understand my anxiety.

Dust swirled around the jeep as thick as the mist around the mountain. I cursed myself for not having a pair of shades like Maria. I caught her smiling at me and I smiled back, hoping she was smiling because she was amused, and not because she thought that I was a complete goof.

"Will you just relax? Here." She moved to her right, producing a thin space beside her, "Squeeze in beside me so you won't get caught on the wires."

"But I'll bounce off."

"No, you won't." Maria gestured to a shapely calf. "Just hook your left foot under that rigging."

I squeezed in beside her and we jostled around for a minute in the cramped space like two puzzle pieces. Finally, she tucked her left side under my right, angled toward me so that I felt her thigh line up with mine, her crotch pressing against my hip, and the side of her left breast resting on my upper arm. I'm sure she didn't notice these things, but I did. Guys always do. I held my breath and counted backwards, trying to calm down.

To fend off fantasies of grabbing her—and being passionately grabbed in return—I decided to talk about something that wasn't arousing in the least.

"So, how long have you been tree planting?"

She laughed, a deep laugh, the kind that belonged to a more mature woman. "Oh, since forever. But we won't be planting this time. Summer's for weeding and watering, or else the saplings we planted last September won't last the season." She paused, then suddenly: "Are you religious, Thomas?"

"Well, I'm Catholic."

"No," she lifted her head to look at me, "I mean, are you devout? Do you pray a lot?"

"I make the sign of the cross before eating."

She laughed again, and once more I had the paranoid fear that she was laughing at me. "Did you know that Nick Joaquin once wrote about our pre-Catholic beliefs? Pagans believed in the union of Mother Earth and her consort every summer solstice. They would commemorate that union during the Beltane fires. Some say the rituals were orgies, but really, they were simply celebrations of both the masculine and feminine deity."

I had started to tune out when she started yakking about "pre-Catholic beliefs". But I perked up again when I heard the word "orgies". I hoped that I wasn't too obvious.

"Those pagans sure had the right idea," was all I managed to reply.

Mang Gerry hit the brakes abruptly, almost dislodging me from the roof. Even before the jeep stopped shuddering, Maria sat up.

"We're here."

When all the packs were set down, Maria introduced me to the other "Eco Friends": Ria, Mars, and Iya. Each girl would handle one group of volunteers. We were each given gardening gloves, shears, and detailed instructions, such as how to differentiate weeds from seedlings. Maria told us to put the weeds in a separate pile.

"Can we smoke them after we collect them?" I asked. I was grinning. Boy, was I witty. She ignored me, but a few of the other male volunteers snickered behind me.

I spent the next two hours bent over the saplings, blinded by my own sweat. I think I snipped a few seedlings along with the weeds, but barely an hour into the activity, I honestly couldn't have cared less.

By lunchtime, everyone was streaked with trails of sweat, or mud, or—as was the case with my arms—some unholy combination of both. Maria worked beside me, and I took every chance I could to sneak peeks at her whenever she bent down. Unlike me, her skin was impeccable—no mud splotches anywhere, just clean, sweet, sweat which I watched run down her shirt. Where my eyes couldn't follow, my imagination had the consideration to take over.

We rinsed off at the river. A few of us bent down by the slabs of flat rock and, after Maria assured us that it was clean, placed our cupped hands under the water rushing through the spaces between. The water was the coolest and freshest I'd ever tasted.

Maria took a dip in the deeper end of the river and came out with her shirt hugging all the right places. She looked like one of those Rogue cover girls, the ones that posed covered in chocolate or wearing nothing but a Philippine flag rendered in body paint. I could imagine Maria covered by a few strategically-placed leaves like a modern day Eve, or painted all green like those wood nymphs in Greek mythology. If I chased her like a horny Apollo, would she turn into a laurel tree? In the photo shoot, her hair would be wildly whipping around her face and her nipples would be erect because of the air condition in the studio.

At lunch, I shared my *adobo* meal with her; she used the spoon, I used the fork. Our utensils collided with each other from time to time. She let me sip some juice from her Nalgene bottle. We watched a group of women downstream, crouched at the edge of the river, wringing newly-washed clothes and beating them with thick pieces of wood.

After lunch, those who didn't want to spend the night on the mountain began the hike down. The remaining male volunteers, Rod, Julian and Carl, began the hike up. The trail was littered with summer's dry batch of cogon and the occasional discarded mini-pack of Boy Bawang. As we trooped through the dense forest, the wrappers crackled under our boot-clad feet, though the girls seemed to barely make a sound.

During the first part of the hike, we would come across men with bolos, women with baskets full of indistinguishable items, and children who would make a mockery of our snail's pace by racing ahead of us barefoot.

"Magandang hapon po," we would greet each as we trudged on. None of them acknowledged our presence as we passed them by. Some acted as if they didn't even see us.

This wasn't to say that everyone ignored our presence on the mountain—a coiled Philippine cobra sunning itself on the trail jerked up when it heard us, muscles taut under its scaly skin, its forked-tongue flickering. Maria was the first to react, although, not in the way I'd expect. She crouched down and arched her back like a cat about to attack and returned the cobra's gaze. Maria hissed at it. The snake jabbed violently at the intervening space, almost touching its snout to her nose, before slithering off the path like a scolded child. "Never break eye contact," was all Maria said.

Another acquaintance that I made during the hike was the friendly limatik which sprang from a leaf and latched onto my arm. Maria wouldn't let me pull it out, saying that its teeth might stay in my skin. So for half an hour I had to watch the creature blow up like a balloon, bloated from feeding on my blood, before it detached and left me bleeding profusely. As she taped my wound, Maria said, "The last person who got bitten bled for two days. That's how strong their anti-coagulant can be." She covered my hand with hers. It was warm and a bit callused. She said, as if she knew that I had a chronic fear of seeing my own blood (I had almost fainted last year when they got a sample for a dengue test), "You'll be fine."

For a moment there I believed her. Three hours later, my pathetic city lungs were screaming for oxygen.

"Straighten up so that the oxygen can circulate better," Maria said as I bent down, resting my hands on my knees and gasping for air so much that I was wheezing. My sweat dripped to the ground.

"Breathe in deeply."

"Rest. Stop?" I gasped.

She laughed again and pointed at the mango tree in the distance. "We can set camp by the bend there."

"We can't all stay in one campsite, there's not enough space," Maria explained. "So Mars and Rod will set up here, Ria and Julian at the clearing over there, Iya and Carl at the next clearing. Thomas, we're right over there."

Maria pulled out the tent's body, fly, and poles. We began setting up the tunnel-shaped tent—I tried to make myself useful by slipping the poles through the appropriate holes and loops.

I took off my sweat-soaked shirt and draped it over the vestibule so that it could dry in the sun. I peeked under my band-aid. I was still bleeding. When I turned back to Maria, she had her sketch pad out and was leisurely doodling. She would glance up at me once in a while with an intense look, then turn back to the sketch pad. I started to feel self-conscious and looked down to examine myself.

I was pale, the kind of pasty-white complexion that you have when you barely get any sun. The day's exposure was already having an effect: an awkward tan was forming on my scraggly arms, turning my bicep into a splotchy half-and-half of red and white. I was scrawnier than a ballet dancer, which meant that my stomach was flat, but lacked the defining lines of a canned tuna TV model.

She was looking at me with a small smile, and again I wondered if she was making fun of me. After a minute she nodded at the page and closed the sketchpad.

"Can I see?" I asked. She couldn't have been sketching for more than five minutes, but when she showed it to me, she had me down to the last detail, even the pathetic sprinkling of whiskers I'd been trying to cultivate into a Van Dyke. She had even drawn the trees behind me in bold, sure strokes. A few layers of pastel colors gave my skin a translucent flesh color, and I seemed like a ghost against that background.

"Wow." It didn't look half bad. Rather, I didn't look half bad. Her lines were wild, and at times, barely there, almost random—but when put together, the overall effect was one of total control.

"Can I see the others?" She handed over the sketch pad and I leafed through pages of charcoal sketches of trees and landscapes drawn with the same technique, broad strokes that created order out of chaos. But there was one drawing that was done with a lighter pencil. The basic form was complete, but it lacked the shading that gave the other images a sense of reality. It was a portrait of a Musang, a wild cat. The animal looked as tame as a house cat, sunning itself by a window, and I wondered if Maria had really sketched one in the wild. The level of detail made me think she had, but I've never seen a wildcat so tame.

When I looked up from the sketchbook, Maria was crouched over a Peak One stove which, judging by its color and rust layers, was probably a million and one years old. She was priming it, her thumb over the hole of the plunger, pumping it in and out with increasing speed. A grunt of exertion escaped her lips. Everything about her was suggestive.

"You have to do this thirty times to compress the air." I certainly wasn't complaining, but when the stove still wouldn't light, she decided to build a fire.

Maria formed a teepee with thin, finger length twigs. She placed three rocks around it and inserted thicker pieces of wood under the twigs. With a bolo in hand, she straddled a stray bamboo chute and squeezed it between her knees. Then she rubbed the bolo edge against the wood, back and forth with a steady rhythm. Watching her, I thought I'd go crazy.

She took the thin, curly bamboo shavings and put them under the teepee. She struck a match, lit the shavings, then bent down and blew a steady stream of air until the fire caught on the twigs. Maria fed the thicker pieces of wood to the growing fire and waited for it to begin to smoke. She then picked up the kaldero, rubbed a bar of soap on the bottom, then filled it with rice and water and propped it on top of the three stones.

Maria brought out materials for cooking dinner: the titanium cook set, the canned goods, oil, onions, garlic and bell peppers. She folded her legs under her arms and watched me from across the fire, her face a mix of light and shadow. For a moment I thought I saw deep wrinkles around her eyes and lips, but that moment came and went, a trick of the light. Though the air around me was still, a breeze seemed to play with her loose hair; it flashed black, then white in the light thrown by the gyrating tongues of flame. Maria took out a bottle of *kwatro kantos* and took a swig before offering me the glass bottle.

"I always imagined the old rituals to be like this." She sidled up to me. "The fire, the priest, the priestess . . . their union . . . the heat of the summer's eve."

I was sweating now. And not from the heat. For lack of something to say, I tipped the bottle to my mouth, drank, and tried to hide my grimace.

"Are you a virgin, Thomas?" She asked.

Of course I was. "No."

The closest I had come to having sex was over the Internet with an Australian girl named Sheila, but I supposed that didn't really count. On the Internet, every Australian girl is named Sheila, and you never know really if she's real. A real girl I mean.

Maria laughed. "I really like you."

She hopped onto my lap, her short shorts riding up, and we started out kissing. I guess I was doing a good job—thank you Internet, alcohol, and FHM—because then she began nibbling my earlobe, working her way south with play bites as soft as a kitten's. She licked my neck, her tongue surprisingly rough. Her fingers unzipped me with a dexterity only obtained through experience. She looked down at me and laughed, but this time I knew it wasn't a mocking laugh. I'd like to think she was pleasantly surprised.

I don't remember much after that; I was in a daze, and mostly sat back and followed her orders. By then, I was used to her taking charge, so when she told me to go down on her, I found myself unsurprised that I suddenly knew exactly what to do, where to probe, what dark caves to explore.

Even after a day of hiking and sweating under the sun, she still smelled like cucumbers, or freshly cut grass. She tasted like the water in the river, cool and clean, and I drank her in and was refreshed.

I do remember how she insisted that I press her against the thick tree beside our tent. She hugged it and dug her nails into the trunk, arching her back and scratching through the bark like a cat against a post. From time to time, she would shush me, warning me that the others might hear, but I don't think she really cared. Quite the opposite really.

She was mewling quietly, and I was panting like a dog behind her when I came the first time. Spent, I noticed the water in the pot boiling over, and the smell of *tutong* in the air—but then we were at it again. Sometime during our second or third go, one of us kicked over the pot and the uneaten rice spilled on the ground, fertilizing the earth it had come from.

At the very end, we slept, skin to skin, in one sleeping bag, poised to emerge like Malakas and Maganda from the heart of the bamboo. Rocks bit into my back through the bag's thin material, and a light shower made the air inside the tent humid and sticky. I buried my face in the nest of her hair. Even in her sleep, Maria's body writhed around like a panther in heat, and with the blood rushing to my erection it took me hours to finally fall asleep. I heard no other sounds but the yowl of mating cats through the night. Sometimes the cat calls sounded almost like human moans, sometimes they sounded like the wind ripping through the fly sheet of our unused tent. I wondered if the other guys were enjoying their camping trip as much as I was.

When I woke up, there was no trace of Maria. There was no sign of a tent, the fire, or of any of the others. Except for my sleeping bag and gear, only a few grains of rice scattered on the ground remained of our campsite. I pulled off the band-aid to see if I was still bleeding. There was no trace of the bite.

I rolled up the sleeping bag, now soaked with the morning dew, stuck it into my bag and prepared for the hours of trekking I had ahead of me. But minutes after I left the campsite, I found myself on a path within walking distance of my cousin's house.

In a bemused state I opened the front door and went straight into Tonton's room. He was lying in bed, reading a textbook on local musical instruments, a highlighter poised to kiss the pages.

"I need a shower." I said, sniffing the air and lifting up my arm.

Tonton looked up. His eyes widened. "Thomas, where have you been? Your dad's been so worried. He thought you went back to Manila, he's been calling all your friends—"

"What? He always overreacts. I was just gone for two days."

Tonton closed his book and stood up, his expression concerned. "You were gone for two weeks, Thomas."

I laughed. "Haha, Tonton. I was gone two days, with that Maria girl from your school. The one that heads the Eco Friends."

Tonton looked confused. "You mean Apple?"

"No man, Maria. Dark, sketches a lot." I scratched at a

mosquito bite. "You should know her." Tonton shook his head again, and I knew his answer even before he gave it.

Maria didn't exist.

I saw her one last time. It had only been less than a year since the camping trip, but a lot had changed. My dad had taken away my video game privileges when I returned to Manila, but I found that I didn't miss them. I started joining other climbs up other mountains: I saw the blanket of clouds above Pulag, experienced the panoramic view of the plains from Arayat, clung to the knife edges of Guiting-Guiting.

Nothing came close to Makiling.

I was half asleep on the bus home from Mt. Cristobal when I had the vision. I was looking out the window when the dark shapes of the passing trees of the expressway slowly blurred and changed. I saw Maria on her back at the very clearing where we'd slept. Her legs were splayed open. Mars, Ria and Iya were there, their bellies heavy and round. A girl was on each side of Maria, and the last knelt in front of her open legs. Maria screamed and her own rounded belly deflated as a cloud of something was expelled from between her legs. It was a while before I realized what the cloud was made of.

Seeds. Millions of tiny seeds.

A violent gust of wind shot through the clearing, and leaves quivered in its wake as it scooped up the seeds and scattered them across the waiting womb of the mountain.

I woke up just as we were passing through Laguna. I was embarrassingly horny. There were seeds floating in the air like dust particles, making the other passengers sneeze. A little girl in the next row opened her hand, chanting "wishy, wishy" as she tried to catch one of the falling, dancing seeds.

I returned my gaze to the window. I could just barely make out the hazy outline of Mt. Makiling. For centuries the mountain had remained unchanged: a woman reclining sensually, mysterious, unconquerable. There was one night when I thought I had conquered her, but I guess that was just my imagination.

HUKLOBAN

The Sorceress Queen

Raissa Rivera Falgui

Raissa Rivera Falgui is a writer of fiction for both children and adults. She has won several awards, including first place for Futuristic Fiction in the 2002 Palanca Awards and second place for short story for children in the 2002 and 2006 Palancas. A member of Kuwentista ng Mga Tsikiting (Kuting), her most recent published stories are for young people, in Tahanan Books' The Night Monkeys and UP Press's Bagets Anthology. She graduated from UP with a degree in Art Studies and is currently working towards an MA in Creative Writing. Over the years, she has worked in various institutions, as English teacher, writer, or editor. Among the most recent jobs she has had was one that required her to write about places she has never visited, including Mt. Malindig in Marinduque. Currently her main job—which she does not plan to give up—is looking after her two children. She is married to an Ateneo English teacher, Joel Falgui.

The Marinduque myth of Maria Malindig is the type of story which leaves us with more questions than answers. In part, that's because of the almost casual mention of the great "Empire of Mu", a name which calls to mind James Churchward's lost continent in the Pacific. Yet, primarily, it's because of the somewhat inconsistent characterization of Maria Malindig herself. How might a powerful queen truly react when confronted with an encroaching patriarchy? Let's find out.

The Emperor of Mu stood on a balcony of his sprawling palace, his eyes taking in the view of the volcano that formed the center of the main island of Mu. The enormous rupture, which so often needed to be tamed by his magical incantations, was at peace for now. Unlike the Emperor's heart.

He was getting old. The long beard that hung down to his feet was now pale gray. Mu tradition dictated that, by his sixtieth year, the Emperor choose his successor from among the other kings of Mu, his closest relations. Traditionally, this was a mere formality, where the other kings swore fealty to the one with the clearest right to the throne. A simple affair, but one sufficient to keep Mu from chaos, for the men of Mu took pride in being men of their word.

This time, if the Emperor had his way, it would not be so simple.

The Northern Kingdom was ruled by his cousin King Laki, strong and robust, yet almost as old as the Emperor. The Southern Kingdom was ruled by King Mannga, likewise aged, and known to be a pompous fool. As for the East . . .

The Emperor's eye fell on a brass sculpture at the corner of the balcony. It was a graceful rendition of a woman, the flowing robes of Mu puddling around her feet, holding a shining ball in one curving hand and a pendulum in the other. The statue also had a more practical purpose: during a tremor, the ball would be struck by the pendulum and land on the bronze skirt with a resounding clang, warning of an impending earthquake.

This clever invention was the work of the Emperor's younger half-brother, Pangkikog, King of the East. Thirty years younger, Mu tradition dictated that Pangkikog was the rightful successor, since the Emperor had no son of his own. But the Emperor had always hated the boy, the favored son, and the thought of Pangkikog inheriting the Empire was too much to bear. The Emperor had never wasted much time with women, considering them weak and foolish. He had focused his energies instead on his study of magic and the rule of the Empire . . . and now, here he was, with his wretched brother as heir to all that he had built. Who was foolish now?

The Emperor looked at the brass sculpture with loathing and struck it with his magical staff. The pendulum knocked the ball from the hand, and the ensuing clang echoed into the palace, low and foreboding.

The Emperor's sixtieth birthday was a lavish celebration. The people gathered before the palace to see the acrobats and dancers perform in the courtyard, which had been opened for the occasion. The Emperor watched in stony silence, then, as the show drew to its end, he stood and raised his hands to still the raucous cheering and clapping. In the silence that followed, all heard him call the names of the three kings. There was much murmuring and speculation among the spectators, even as Laki, Mannga, and Pangkikog strode forth to make their obeisance to the Emperor.

From his high throne, the Emperor made his declaration: "Knowledge of magical arts, the source of our strength, is dying across the Empire. None of the possible successors has been found to be capable of sorcery. We must then renew the imperial bloodline with a sorceress as mighty as myself to be the helpmate of the new emperor. He who can find and win a bride with such power shall be decreed my heir."

The two older kings squared their shoulders and stared impassively at the crowd, many of whom seemed amused at the thought of the old men going courting. The people knew that courtship amongst royalty was about more than charm: it was Imperial Edict that a King of Mu could only marry a woman he had won by right of challenge, one which was often physical in nature. As for the youngest King, Pangkikog smiled as he made his obeisance. He already had someone in mind.

Queen Maryam of the Kingdom of Malindig was known far and wide for her power and beauty. While already twice the age that most girls in her kingdom became brides, she still looked young, with smooth bronze skin and long, flowing black hair. Her dark eyes were like polished stone, reflecting, it was whispered, the hardness of her heart. Perhaps this was why nobody had ever declared love for her or tried to woo her as in the tales of old. In private, this fact caused her to seethe with fury. What good was beauty if it didn't bring men to their knees, and force them into foolhardy contests for her hand?

After her victory in the war that had claimed her father's life, Maryam had assumed the throne. She knew her cold, harsh father had not been loved, and she basked in the cheers of the people, hearing adulation in their hopeful cries. Her first act as monarch was to invite unmarried warriors, those who had distinguished themselves in the campaign, to select their reward. One by one they presented themselves before her, and Maryam gave two choices to each: a chest with a small sum of gold, no more than a year's wages, or Maryam's hand in marriage.

To a man, the young soldiers chose the gold. Some already had sweethearts and chose to be faithful; others feared her mysterious powers; yet others, her temper. All made their excuses, claimed that their family had need of gold, that they were not worthy of the queen.

Maryam had cared nothing for their reasons. Each of those who rejected her was turned to smoke by the sorceress queen's magical wand.

Now, Maryam waited in bitter and lonely silence as the full moon rose and cast its pale rays on the unruffled waters of the scrying pool. When enough light had penetrated the waters, Maryam touched her magic staff gently to the surface and compelled the pool to reveal images of events that were of import to her and her kingdom.

The waters reflected a most curious scene: three ships, with brightly colored sails, each commanded by a man of fine stature, brilliantly robed and surely royal in his bearing. Three ships, making their way to her island, bearing men worthy of her hand.

Maryam then touched the surface of the pool again, muttering an incantation. The sky grew dark and the wind rose with a menacing whistle. She raised her arms to conduct the winds, to summon a typhoon that blew the sea toward Malindig from every direction.

The next morning dawned calm and clear, and the people of Malindig, after a collective sigh of relief, set to work surveying and repairing the damage caused by the strange, sudden typhoon. However, many a man who climbed up on his roof to patch it was diverted by a magical sight—three ships raising their brilliant sails to sweep up to the shore of the island kingdom. From her high marble tower, Maryam of Malindig sent forth an eagle to circle above the three boats, as they anchored by the shore. In a small scrying glass she held in her hand, she could see through the eagle's eyes and noted with satisfaction that one of the men was of an age with her, and rather handsome, with a noble bearing.

The general of Maryam's army, afraid that the strange, important-looking men on the beach might be foreign invaders, assembled his men and marched them to the shore. Shadowed by curious civilians, the general confronted the three grandly dressed men, demanding that they identify themselves.

Laki spoke first. In ringing, arrogant tones, he introduced them as the greatest kings of Mu.

"And what is your purpose on our shores?" demanded the general.

"Word of your queen's beauty and power has reached the empire of Mu. We come here seeking her hand in marriage." He conveniently left out the fact that he and Mannga had been merely tailing Pangkikog, and had only recently learned of their ultimate destination.

At the King's words, there was a loud cheer from the people. With their eyes on the chests of gifts the kings' retainers carried, the people appealed to the general to lead the kings to the palace right away.

As they approached the palace, the kings were disappointed to see that the architecture of the island consisted mainly of rough huts. "And the women are so ugly," Laki complained. "Can we really be certain the queen is as lovely as they say?"

Mannga chuckled, but Pangkikog strode on and said nothing. Though most of the women who went about uncovered were harsh of feature, he saw many a pair of luxurious dark eyes peer at him from behind a veil. He was sure he would find hidden loveliness in these rustic homes if he desired to seek it, but his thoughts were all for the mystical Maryam of Malindig.

Pangkikog had heard of the queen through the merchant seamen of his kingdom. He had a great interest in foreign trade and befriended the most successful merchants, inviting them to the palace to dine with him that he might learn more about their concerns and the foreign lands they traded in. It was through these merchants that he learned of the wealthy kingdom of Malindig and its queen. Like most, Pangkikog had heard much of Maryam's beauty and the harshness of her rule—but unlike most, he had also heard stories which made him confident that there was more to the sorceress than her terrible power.

Soon, the palace was before them, a shimmering white structure decorated with patterned tiles that glistened with a myriad of changing colors. A little distance from it stood a tower that soared to the heavens. At last, here were sights worthy of the enchanted land of Mu, proof of its queen's power.

When they came before the queen, each of the men was struck mute by her beauty. Pankikog, seeing her cold, hard eyes, felt pity for her and cleared his throat, but Laki found his voice first. In his flattering tone, the eldest King declared: "We have come here that we might ask for your hand, O beautiful queen." And he flung open a cache full of gold.

Maryam of Malindig, dripping with intricate gold jewelry from head to toe, glanced at its contents and was bored. She peered at Mannga's offerings of ivory carvings with more interest, but then her eyes reached Pangkikog's chest, where they lingered. The youngest King took the time to explain each item to her, as she stroked the silks and sniffed the perfumed oils. The queen clapped her hands. A dozen servants marched in, bearing gold and silver platters laden with food. Looking into Pangkikog's eyes, she announced, "First, we shall feast."

Laki took the seat directly opposite the queen to show himself her equal in rank. But the other two men approached the seats on either side of the queen, determined to speak to her and win her heart.

Yet Mannga could say but little, distracted by the numerous delicacies of the feast. While he gorged himself on the fresh spiced shrimps, salads of dark green forest ferns and seaweed, and crab cooked in a sauce of roe, Laki alternated between complimenting the feast and bragging about his accomplishments. But Maryam inclined her ear more to Pangkikog, who spoke with fervor of his beloved land of Mu and his dreams for it.

By the time the creamy coconut-sprinkled cakes and platters of sweet fruit were brought in, the queen had satisfied herself that she had seen into each man's heart. She rose and declared: "I have made my choice. Pangkikog is the king on whom I choose to bestow my hand."

Laki rose in anger, knocking over golden goblets of wine as he leaned across the table and roared, "That cannot be! It is written in the laws of our land that a king of Mu can only marry a woman whom he has won in a fair contest."

Maryam glowered. "A queen of Malindig, however, does as she pleases, and it pleases me to marry King Pangkikog."

King Mannga addressed Pangkikog across the table in pompous tones. "You know our tradition. To do otherwise would be to dishonor both our stations and the queen's. Would you bring such shame upon us?"

Pangkikog bristled. "I would not be a worthy successor of the empire of Mu if I were not to win my bride in a challenge." He bowed to the queen and said, "My queen, I must adhere to the edict of my own land."

"Very well, then," replied the queen, "A race. Yes, a race between your ships, first thing in the morning, for the privilege of my hand. And now you will be escorted to your rooms."

Pangkikog slept that night rocked on the waves of blissful of dreams, dreams of holding his mysterious queen in his arms, running his hands over her graceful curves. She wore the silken robe he had brought her, purple like his sails, and it flowed sensuously over his thighs as he thrust into her, struggling to break through. His fingers dug into warm flesh and blood, and his eyes flung open. The queen was there in bed with him, her robe falling from her shoulders, revealing her heated body dewed with perspiration. Frustrated passion smoldered in her eyes.

This was no dream. Pangkikog drew away.

"My lady," he said with a great effort. He was no longer touching her, but it was impossible to refrain from gazing at her graceful form that gleamed as bronze as the sculptures he'd created. Seeing his eyes travel down her body, the queen smiled.

"I and my kingdom could be yours forever, with certainty, without contest," she purred. "Would you risk all that by adhering to a meaningless tradition?"

"It has meaning for me," he replied with as much dignity as a man could, with his hardness poorly shielded by a fine white sheet. "I gave my word."

"Then you will exert yourself to the utmost to make certain of your victory, will you not?" she said, pressing her palms against his muscular chest and sinuously drawing her body against his.

Pangkikog drew his hand gently down her back, cupping her curves. "Ah, what a prize I shall bring home to the empire of Mu. A beautiful consort to reign by my side."

The queen's tongue traveled up his neck, ending at the lobe of his ear. "After our visit to Mu we shall return here, of course, for you are to rule my kingdom beside me."

His hand grazed her side as he reached up and stroked her breast with one masterful thumb, making her moan and shudder. "Your kingdom shall become part of the empire of Mu, and we shall visit it to administer it. But the Empire of Mu must be our home. Mu is everything to me," he explained. "I have devoted my life to the improvement of my own kingdom, all for the glory of Mu"

"Are you ... to be ... emperor ... then?" she gasped, amidst the little cries of pleasure that his caresses elicited from her.

"If I succeed in winning your hand, yes."

The queen pushed his hand away and drew back from him.

"So that is all I am to you, a prize, a tribute, to be presented in order to win the imperial seat?"

"To me, you are not," he said, soothingly. "You are, to me, a beautiful queen, the queen of my heart. I know you. I know something of what it feels to grow up in a household of hatred, where those who share your blood pray for your death." Pangkikog felt her soften at his words, and, emboldened, he continued. "You want what is best for your people, and I can give you that. Your kingdom will be a part of my Empire, and it will prosper as surely as any other land over which I have ruled."

Maryam stiffened. "You ask me to give up my kingdom."

"To become part of an empire."

"And what shall I be in your empire?"

"My beautiful consort, assisting and advising me, wielding your magic as I determine the need for it. And I shall wield my own brand of magic on you."

He reached for her slender waist and his right hand traveled down her front, his thumb sliding down to stroke her moist and tender regions below till she threw her head back and shrieked. He leaned forward, teasing her nipple with his tongue. "Lie down, my queen, and let me possess you entirely," he panted.

At his words, his commanding tone, trembling as she was, Maryam opened her eyes. "A queen of Malindig throws herself down before no one," she declared. Shaky yet resolute, she rose. Looking down upon him, she said: "I trust then, that you are determined to win this contest, for more reasons than one. When you have won, I suppose that there will be time enough to discuss the terms of our union."

"Indeed," he said, bowing his head. "Perhaps it is too presumptuous of us to celebrate my victory beforehand, certain though I am of it."

Maryam saw the frustration in his eyes and smiled. She would forgive him, of course. It would have been different if it had been one of the others.

"I shall not marry either of the other kings, should they win over you," she declared.

"It is against the laws of Mu—"

"It is not against my laws, however." She clutched her robe around her, tossing her head.

"In any case, I shall not entertain the thought of losing," Pangkikog said.

"I suppose if you lose you shall be dishonored?" she said slowly. He nodded, and the Queen's tone turned speculative. "If that were so, know that you would be welcome to remain here. In my land, only my laws need apply. And yours, should you choose to remain with me."

Her hand slid down, letting her robe fall partly open. He gazed at her in silence, which she took for assent. Smiling, the queen swept triumphantly out of the room.

In the morning, each of the kings was aided by servants to bathe and dress, then bade to step on a small rug. Each found himself carried out to the sea, to his own ship which was anchored a good distance from the shore.

"We must race into the arms of the queen, I suppose," Pangkikog said to himself. But before he set sail, he paused to think.

He knew the other kings well, and decided he must take advantage of each man's weakness. Laki was arrogant. Mann-ga did not think much of Pangkikog, and would focus solely on striving to beat Laki. Pangkikog decided his best strategy would be to lag behind for the better part of the race, then unsettle his two opponents by suddenly speeding up. Pondering thus, he let the two others have a generous head start, while he paused to watch an eagle circling above him.

The members of the court had the best vantage point, high in the tower of Maryam of Malindig. The ladies who attended the Queen whispered among each other, glancing over their shoulders at Maryam, wondering why she sat looking at herself in a mirror instead of joining them at the balcony to view the progress of the race. But then the Queen was known to be vain, and that might account for her intent study of the little mirror in the shape of an eye. Perhaps it was for the best, the ladies whispered, for they feared how the Queen would react to see her favored one fare so poorly.

Everyone could see that Pangkikog's boat lagged behind, while Laki's and Mannga's were neck and neck. It did not seem likely the youngest King would win. Everyone glanced surreptitiously at the Queen to see her reaction. Still looking into the mirror, she was frowning deeply. Then she closed her eyes for a moment. When she opened them again, her expression was pleased, almost triumphant.

Some thought, seeing this change in her face, that she had given Pangkikog some kind of magical assistance, and strained to see what change had occurred. For a time, nothing magical seemed to happen—then came the excited cries: "Look, your Majesty, look!"

The morning of the contest dawned with the Queen in quite the state. The more she thought of this Mu tradition, the more unsettled she became. She was not a trophy to possess. She was beginning to contemplate the prospect of humiliating the three men who were fighting for the right to possess her. They would return to Mu with tales of her might . . .

But then the contest began and the Queen noticed Pangki-kog's laggard pace. Maryam's first reaction was one of fury. Was he so poor a seaman? Was he exerting no effort? Did he not want her any longer? Then she remembered their conversation last night. Of course. He was accepting the compromise she offered.

The Queen allowed herself a smile. Then came the excited cries of her ladies.

"Your Majesty, the young king is winning! Pangkikog is beating the others to the shore." They looked at her expectantly.

To the members of the court, Maryam seemed not to respond, for she simply lowered her eyes to her mirror. Then she shrieked and rose to her feet. The ladies gasped as the Queen flung down her small silver mirror in a fury and raced down the spiraling stairs of the tower.

In her chamber, Maryam seized her magical staff. She swept out of the palace and strode to the beach, her robes fluttering around her in a wind that rose with her fury. Who was Pangkikog to think that she was less than him? Pangkikog was still some distance away, but she could see in his stance the confidence, the determination . . . and at that point the Queen realized what was truly important to her.

"No man shall possess me or my kingdom!" she cried. She whipped her hair back defiantly, raised her staff, and called all the elements to do her bidding.

High in the pure white tower that Maryam of Malindig had built, the people of the court were witness to the destruction of the kingdom. The ladies clutched each other as the tower shook along with the ground, the very earth undulating, and cracking, swept over by mighty waves that swallowed people, houses, and trees before their frightened eyes.

They saw the boats of Laki and Mannga collide into each other and capsize. Then they saw the boat with the purple sails—now lowered—ride towards the shore with the waves, its lone occupant clinging to its mast. Was this the Queen's way of assuring his win? But then the enormous wave rolled back, and the royal ship was thrown with amazing force, flinging its lone occupant into the furious sea.

The Queen threw back her head, screaming with laughter. Then, as the enormous wave that caused Pangkikog's demise returned to sweep back over the shore, the sorceress Queen vanished beneath the mighty swell.

When the final wave had ebbed, three new islands were visible at sea, and on land, where Maryam's palace had once stood, was a mountain with a steep and elegant peak, from whence issued scalding steam. In the stillness that followed the calamity, no sound could be heard, but in the ears of all who yet survived echoed the laughter of Maryam of Malindig.

The traders brought back the tragic news from Malindig weeks later. They had seen the changed land with their own eyes, navigated around the islets, one of which had been made a graveyard. The survivors had named it Laki, the king they believed responsible for the final challenge and all that followed.

With the knowledge that its kings would never return, the Empire of Mu was torn apart by civil strife. Gradually, families began to depart from the war-torn empire, seeking quiet tropical isles where they could live in peace. Today, no record of the great Empire remains.

As for Malindig, now Marinduque, few remember its sorceress Queen. Those who do tell a different tale of her end, one of a lovelorn virgin or one who sinned against the gods. But those who know the truth know why Mount Malindig, the volcano that rose from the rubble of Maryam's kingdom, has never erupted. To this day, it holds back, merely seething hot water.

ᜋᜃᜉᜆᜄ᜔ | ᜋᜎᜂᜈ᜔

MAKAPATAG / MALAON

Beneath the Acacia

Celestine Trinidad

Celestine Trinidad is a newly licensed physician who still tries to read and write as much as she can in her (now unfortunately very little) free time. Her stories have appeared in other publications such as Philippine Genre Stories, Philippine Speculative Fiction IV, Philippines Free Press, and Usok. Much to her own surprise, she won the Don Carlos Palanca Memorial Award for Literature in 2008 for her short story for children "The Storyteller and the Giant."

Maria Sinukuan, guardian of Arayat, is one of the mountain goddesses, like the more famous Maria Makiling. Unlike her counterpart from Makiling, however, Maria Sinukuan is much less generous with her affections—"Sinukuan" means "Unconquerable", and she frequently uses her wits to extricate herself from unwanted suitors. In this young adult tale, Maria—along with a particularly persistent suitor—gets to apply her wit in another way, in order to solve a mystery.

    After a long voyage on foot through several villages, towns, forests, and mountain ranges, he finally arrived outside the court of the goddess Maria Sinukuan, only to find himself faced with another obstacle: a throng of villagers from the town to the west of Mount Arayat, all standing before the gates of the palace of the goddess. Still, he went on, elbowing his way through the crowd, happily oblivious to the glares and threats of the crowd around him. He heard someone threaten him with disembowelment, and someone else swore to suspend him upside down for three whole days atop the highest tree in the forest, but he did not stop until he came face-to-face with an old man. The old man smiled through his gray, bushy beard, looking amused.

"Young men these days," the man said. "Always in a hurry. You are not from here, are you?"

"Here?" The young man blinked, as if seeing the crowd around him for the first time. He stood out from the crowd, with his bare feet, much-mended and worn-out *camisa* and trousers, and the twigs and leaves sticking out of his black unruly hair. "From your town? No. I only came here to see Maria."

The man chuckled, holding up a hand as the crowd around them gasped in collective horror. "I can see that you are indeed not from here," he said. "No one would dare to call the Lady Sinukuan so . . . informally. They call me Mang Andres, and I am a farmer from the town to the west. What is your name, boy?"

The young man tilted his head to one side, looking thoughtful. "Juan," he said after a moment's pause.

"Very well, Juan," Mang Andres said. "What did you come here to the Lady Sinukuan's court for?"

"To marry Maria," Juan said, matter-of-factly.

There were more gasps from the crowd, and Mang Andres sighed. "No, no. Were you not warned about this?" He pointed to a group of men kneeling before the gates, carrying flowers and gifts in their arms. "They are much like you, men who love the Lady Sinukuan, but to no avail. They beg, plead, and threaten to take their lives if she refuses them—but to all of them the good Lady only shakes her head, and gently, but firmly, closes the palace gates, ignoring all their cries. Some young men move on and marry other women, but most of them just waste away in their longing. Alas, the Lady Sinukuan is always unmoved."

"But she will marry me," Juan insisted.

"So everyone else says, young man," said Mang Andres. "You are no different. In any case, she has no time to listen to you, for she has other concerns. See those people over there?"

The young man's eyes idly followed where Mang Andres pointed, to a group of tall warriors standing guard over men and women with chains on their wrists. "Those in chains are criminals," the old man said, "and the Lady Sinukuan passes judgment on them. She determines who is truly innocent, and what punishment to give to the guilty. She is sometimes ruthless. No one knows exactly what happens to these men, for they return from their sentences changed, always looking back at the Lady's mountain with fear in their eyes. Some say these are the ones she transforms into wild pigs, for a time. Others never return. Some believe they are sentenced to wander the forests . . . forevermore." The old man's voice dropped into a whisper, and he leaned forward. "You would not want to anger the Lady Sinukuan."

"What is that for?" Juan said, pointing to a garland of garlic bulbs strewn around the head of one woman, who glared back at them with red eyes.

"That," Mang Andres said grimly, "Is to keep her from using her power."

Interest finally lit up in the young man's eyes.

"Yes," Mang Andres said, "That woman is an *enkanto*, a creature of the night. She is a *manananggal*. She is able to sprout wings and remove the upper half of her body from the lower. She flies into the town at night, and feeds on the townspeople as they sleep. She was captured for the death of one of the townsmen, who they found two mornings ago with all his insides missing. The garlic is to keep her from dividing herself and escaping—"

"There is no need for that," Juan said, and the spark of interest in his eyes died.

"Why do you say so?"

"Because she cannot transform during the day," said Juan, and Mang Andres raised an eyebrow. "Besides, she is innocent. Two nights ago wasn't a full moon. There is one thing most people forget about beings like her: that they can only transform and hunt on the night of the full moon. It is only logical, after all. If they did so every night, then no one in your town would be left alive."

"That is true," the old man said thoughtfully. "And this is the first time I've ever heard of a *manananggal* actually killing one of the townspeople. But there can be no other—"

"And they rarely feed on humans now," Juan continued, "Since you have found ways to protect yourselves against them. One of your townsmen committed the murder, and made it look as if she did it. Maria will let her go free too, I'm sure of that."

Mang Andres stood frowning after some time, and finally he shook his head. "It is true that the Lady Sinukuan is far too relenting to these *enkantos*," he said. "But I think it unwise. These creatures are afraid of her now, but someday—" His voice trailed off.

He took something from his pocket, and pressed it into the young man's hand. It was a wooden amulet, with inscriptions on its oval front face: *evil be gone*, it said in prominent *baybayin* characters. "It can't hurt to be safe, after all. There are many of them in this forest. Cigar-smoking *kapres* hide in the treetops, waiting to jump on you; a harmless deer could turn out to be an *aswang*, and eat you up when you least expect it; or, while you walk through the forests at night, a *tikbalang* could suddenly crush you under its hoofs—one of my neighbors saw one last night, as a matter of fact. Take this amulet. It will protect you."

Before Juan could thank him, the palace gates suddenly opened, and Maria Sinukuan herself appeared before them. Her long black hair, reaching up to the hem of her long white dress, shone in the rapidly brightening light of the sunrise.

The crowds flocked around her, but she held her hand up, and they stopped in their tracks.

"I cannot stay," she said, and Juan sighed at the sound of her voice: it was gentle, melodious, as pleasant as a bird's song; yet it contained a power that seemed to hold him fast by his ankles, binding him to where he stood. "I have to leave to look into a most important matter. But I will be back to settle your concerns soon." She looked at the woman with red eyes Juan was watching earlier, and she said, "Set her free at once: she is innocent. If you wish for an explanation, I suggest you wait here until I get back."

There were some murmurs from the crowd, but the Lady Sinukuan only smiled at them. "Mang Andres," she called, and the man stood up, startled, "I need to speak to you about your daughter."

With a smile and a nod at Juan, Mang Andres followed after the Lady Sinukuan. After a moment's thought, Juan trailed after them, his bare feet making no sound as he ran.

"You truly are kind, dear Lady, in doing this for my daughter," Mang Andres said, looking back at the townspeople. "And you knew even before I was able to speak to you! But of course, you know everything." He smiled at the Lady Sinukuan, but she did not return his smile. She only looked at him, a great sadness in her eyes. "But I do not wish to trouble you further. Just tell me where she is, and I will bring her back myself."

"Mang Andres," the Lady Sinukuan said gently. "You cannot bring your daughter back. It is far too late."

"Why?"

"She is dead. I'm really sorry."

At that moment, the whole forest hushed. The birds suddenly ceased their singing, and the wind died down, no longer rustling through the leaves of the trees. Not a sound could be heard, except for Mang Andres' voice, as he said, in a voice barely above a whisper, "Why?"

"I do not know," Maria Sinukuan said, and the forest came back to life once more. She closed her eyes. "But I cannot feel her, not anymore. I *did* feel something amiss about your daughter's death, however, which is why I have set out with you. I sensed that she felt great anguish as she died . . . suffering. Too much suffering. I'm afraid someone may have murdered her."

"*Murdered?*"

"I have sent my seekers to find her, and they have sharper eyes than the townspeople, so they shall find her soon. In the meantime, I would like you to tell me what happened."

"But . . ." Mang Andres sank to his knees. "All they will find is not my daughter, but a corpse. I cannot believe that she—"

"When did you last see your daughter?" Juan suddenly interrupted, and the Lady Sinukuan looked at him in surprise.

"I—I—" Mang Andres swallowed before speaking. "Y-yesterday morning. We were arguing about her impending marriage, and then she—" He choked back his tears. "She left. I thought she would be back by the evening, but she did not return, so this morning I went to see the Lady Sinukuan."

"Could you take us to your house?" Juan said.

The Lady Sinukuan stepped forward then. The only hint of her displeasure came from the sudden pursing of her lips, and yet Juan felt the full force of her anger, almost as if she had raised her hand and grabbed him by the throat.

"I believe it is not your place to be so familiar, being a stranger here," she said. "Who are you, young man?"

Juan looked up to meet her gaze. "My name is Juan," he

said. "I came here to marry you, Maria."

The Lady Sinukuan stepped back, and after a few moments of staring incredulously at him, began to laugh imperiously. "Marry me?" she said, looking at him with a mixture of pity and scorn, "I believe I never gave you any permission to do so—"

"But there are other matters at hand," Juan continued as if he did not hear her, "We shall discuss this some other time, Maria. For now there is the death of Mang Andres' daughter. Could you take us to your home, Mang Andres?" The man nodded blankly. "Straight ahead? All right, let's go."

The Lady Sinukuan and Mang Andres ran to catch up with the young man, who, in a matter of seconds, was already some distance ahead of them. He did not walk, but went along in a sort of gallop, once even kicking up so much dust from the path that the Lady Sinukuan had to summon a breeze to keep her and Mang Andres from choking.

They finally stopped before a large wooden house, much like the other houses nearby, with a roof of *nipa*, *capiz*-paned windows, and a small veranda looking out into the fields beyond. Juan squinted, and saw rice and corn stalks growing in the field, still young, waiting for harvest time.

"I—I'm sorry I wasn't able to prepare for your visit," Mang Andres said brokenly, "I never thought that—"

"What happened to that tree?" Juan interrupted, pointing to their left, to a stump of a tree blackened by fire just a few feet away.

"I had to cut it down," Mang Andres said, only sparing a small glance at the tree stump, "We were going to build my daughter's new house there."

"What happened to your hand, young man?" The Lady Sinukuan asked in turn, staring at the young man's palm, but Juan quickly closed his hand into a fist and shook his head.

"It's nothing," Juan said, "I suffered a burn . . . just like this tree was burned, before Mang Andres cut it down. Am I right?" When the man nodded absently, Juan walked over to the tree stump, and came back minutes later, carrying some ash from the tree stump, a small charred branch, and a blackened flower. "Look at this, Maria," he said, but the Lady Sinukuan ignored him, intent on the newcomer that had joined them during his absence.

Beside her now stood a tall man carrying an axe in one hand and tree logs in the other. He was frowning at Mang Andres, his thick black eyebrows meeting together at the center of his wide forehead.

"Victoria," he was saying, "I—I cannot believe it."

"Yes," said Mang Andres, and this time, he was weeping. "I'm really sorry, Florante. We still don't know what happened to her, but the lady Sinukuan is doing all she can to help us."

"But what about all that money for the house?" Florante said, his grip on his axe tightening.

"These things you should not worry about," the Lady Sinukuan said. She frowned at him, and put one hand on one of the logs he was carrying. "The young lady that you love is dead."

"Well—yes, yes," Florante said, glancing behind him, then looking back at Mang Andres. "This is most unfortunate. I—I have to go now."

At this, he turned, resting the handle of his axe on his shoulder as he walked away.

"Poor Florante," Mang Andres said. "To lose his betrothed before the wedding. My poor child!" And he continued to sob, while the Lady Maria continued to watch Florante, until he disappeared from view.

"Interesting," Juan said, tilting his head towards Maria. "Shouldn't we go inside the house now, Maria? We shall certainly learn nothing more standing here outside."

The Lady Sinukuan's eyes narrowed, and her lips quivered with suppressed annoyance, but she only said, "Mang Andres, would you permit us to go inside your home? You can tell us everything inside."

Mang Andres led them into his home, and they sat down on bamboo chairs surrounding the table at the center of the room. Juan looked intently at the portraits hanging on the wall behind where the Lady Sinukuan was seated, and she turned in her seat to look at them as well.

"I remember your wife," she said, running her hand over the portrait of Mang Andres, his wife, and his daughter, "She came to me to ask me to bless the child she carried in her womb."

"She was never very strong," Mang Andres said, "but she fought to keep our child, and died giving her life. Fortunately, Victoria turned out to be a strong child, and grew up to be a capable woman. And now, just when she was about to become a mother herself, she . . ."

"Mang Andres," the Lady Sinukuan said, looking at him gravely. "There is something I must ask you, and I hope that you will not be offended by this."

"It's all right, Lady Sinukuan," said Mang Andres, managing a smile, "You can ask anything."

"Florante did not love Victoria, did he?" She smiled sadly when Mang Andres jumped to his feet, startled. "Yes, I suspected as much. The marriage was arranged, then?"

"Our families have always been good friends," Mang Andres said, sitting back down. "Victoria and Florante grew up together, so when we talked about the marriage, the two children did not raise any objections. It was only when we started planning the house for them that the trouble with my daughter started . . ."

"This was the argument you spoke of?" Juan finally spoke.

"Yes," Mang Andres said. "We had been arguing for quite

some time now. The only place where we can build her house was where the acacia tree once stood, but she refused to have it cut down."

"Acacia," Juan echoed, looking thoughtful. "I see."

"Oh, do be quiet," the Lady Sinukuan snapped. "Mang Andres, please continue."

"I told her we had to, if she wanted to have a house built, but she was very adamant about it," Mang Andres said. "And then—yesterday morning, she told me that she wanted to have their marriage called off completely. I—I said things I regret now, and she left, never to return . . ."

"Did she not love Florante as well, then?"

"She thought he was very kind," Mang Andres said. "And liked his company, at the very least."

The Lady Sinukuan stood up suddenly, looking at something outside the window. "Pardon me, but I have to go outside for a moment. No, no, you need not stand up—I shall go alone."

She slipped out the door, her long skirt trailing behind her.

She was greeted by a flock of *maya* birds, twittering happily. One of them came down to rest on her outstretched hand.

Have you found her? she asked the bird inside her palm, although she did not speak.

No, my Lady.

But that can't be. She must still be somewhere—

We searched the whole town, my Lady, and all of the towns of Pampanga.

And the ants saw nothing? Or the worms? The fish from the rivers?

Nothing, my Lady.

Very well. You may rest for a while, but I would like you to continue the search. She scattered some seeds on the ground for the rest of the flock, and set the *maya* in her hand down on the ground with the others.

She reentered the house, and sat down before the portraits once more. "Did your daughter have any relations with anyone from the other towns? Did you ever bring her with you outside the town?"

"No, Lady Sinukuan," Mang Andres said. "She stayed in this town all her life."

"And no visitors from the other towns took an interest in her? Or would even wish her harm?"

"No, Lady Sinukuan," Mang Andres said again, this time with a note of incredulity in his voice. "Everyone loved her. She had many friends, but only from this town. And she had no enemies. Why do you ask?"

"Because," she said, "It seems that your daughter is nowhere to be found in this town, or in the nearby towns."

"But why would—" Mang Andres looked confused. "It's impossible."

"I think she attempted to run farther away than you imagined," the Lady Sinukuan murmured, "And there she met her end, somewhere in the neighboring provinces. Or someone else carried her body there in order to hide the crime. I will have more seekers search for her, but I doubt if we will have any news of her by tonight."

"I . . . I see," Mang Andres said hollowly. "Thank you for all your trouble, Lady Sinukuan. I think you should go back to your palace now, for you have done more than enough for us. You have other matters to attend to . . ."

"I will stay for the moment," the Lady Sinukuan said, shaking her head. "There is still a suspicion I have to lay to rest. Until that is done, I shall wait here."

"Wait for what, Lady Sinukuan?"

"Wait for my watcher to return to me," she said. She looked around, and said, "Why, where is that young man who was with you?"

"Juan?" Mang Andres looked around too, surprised. "I didn't realize that he had gone."

The Lady Sinukuan cast an eye around the room, and her gaze fell on the stairs. She bent down and picked up a wooden amulet lying on the first step.

"Will you permit me to go upstairs, Mang Andres?" she said.

"Of course," Mang Andres nodded. "Those are the rooms where we sleep. My daughter has the left room, while mine is the one to the right."

"Thank you, Mang Andres."

The Lady Sinukuan ascended the stairs, and found that the door to the left was slightly ajar.

"*What*," she exclaimed, upon entering the room, "in Bathala's name, are you *doing*?"

Juan was half-buried in the sheets that covered the young lady's bed, putting one end of the blanket to his nose and sniffing it carefully. He dived under the sheets and surfaced again, carrying one piece of the bedsheet, torn from one end.

"The lady Victoria has a very soft bed," he said absent-mindedly, "Would you care to join me here, Maria?"

"I have had enough!" Maria threw up her hands, and a strong gust of wind swept through the room, toppling him off the bed. "I do not know who you are and where you came from, and why you would even *presume* that I would marry a mere mortal like you, but you cannot continue to show me this disrespect—"

"Oh, calm down, darling," Juan said, and Maria's eyes widened at the remark, but he suddenly jumped out of the bed, and slipped out the door.

"That *man*!" she cried in exasperation before following him out the door.

Juan had gone down to Mang Andres, and had just asked him a question Maria did not hear. The older man's reaction to the question was very odd: his eyes widened, and a bead of sweat rolled down his forehead.

"But what does . . . *that* . . . have to do with . . ."

A flash of color from the window caught the Lady Sinukuan's attention, and after telling Juan explicitly not to say anything else while she was gone, she went out the door. After a few minutes, she gestured from outside the window for the two men to follow her.

They followed her, and saw her releasing a butterfly that had been perched on her finger. It did not fly away, however, but remained to flutter around her skirt.

"My watcher has returned," she said, a look of satisfaction on her face. "And she told me of what I had suspected in the first place."

"And what was that, Maria?" Juan said, smiling.

"Florante," she said. "I hid my watcher beneath one of the tree logs he was carrying earlier, and she heard everything. Apparently, Florante's family is coming to ruin, and in a year, they will have nothing else left. But you, Mang Andres, you are doing quite well, as Victoria has managed your finances quite capably. This is why the impending marriage was a great convenience for Florante's family: they wanted your money. It is a story I have heard countless times."

"Florante?" Mang Andres shook his head. "I knew they were falling upon terrible times, which is why I said that I would shoulder all the expenses for the house. But he would never do this. And his father would never—no, Julio would never—"

"Desperation can drive men to far worse deeds, Mang Andres," the Lady Sinukuan said gravely. "My watcher told me that they were discussing their plans for their future. They would make off with all the money you gave them for the house you were having built, and start anew in another province, far away from your vengeance. But they cannot escape my wrath."

Her eyes started glowing, lit by blue fire glowing from within. Juan suddenly grabbed her by the wrist and said, "We mustn't be too hasty, Maria."

Maria pulled her hand back, and even Mang Andres looked scandalized; it was a breach of conduct to touch a woman, much less the Lady Sinukuan. "You better explain yourself," she hissed, the light in her eyes still glowing.

"They are indeed guilty of wishing to steal Mang Andres' money," Juan said, and he looked at the butterfly still fluttering around Maria. "I'm not questioning what you heard," he said to it, then turned back to Maria. "They were, however, innocent of the murder of his daughter. Why kill her when they could have received twice as much from her alive, rather than dead? It doesn't make any sense."

"Then who did?" Mang Andres said. "And what does *it* have to do with this whole matter?"

"It?" The Lady Sinukuan raised an eyebrow.

"The one who lives in that acacia tree," Juan explained. "The *kapre*."

The Lady Sinukuan stared first at Mang Andres, who visibly paled, then to Juan, who was looking at the other man expectantly.

"Was that not the reason why she did not want you to cut down that acacia tree?" Juan went on, "and why you burned the tree down in anger, when your daughter did not come back in the evening? Because he caused this whole problem with your daughter?"

"You burned down my home?"

It was a terrible voice that spoke: like the sound of waves crashing onto a shore, crushing rocks into fine sand with its force. Mang Andres flinched, while Maria and Juan looked up at the mango tree above them, where a horrible apparition stood among the branches, blocking out the light from the sun.

It was a tall, tall man; taller than the entire first floor of the house behind them. His yellowed teeth stood out from the shadows, a large cigar sticking out between them.

"So *you* were the one?" the *kapre* bellowed. "I suspected, but because of the love your daughter and I had for each other, I wanted to be sure—"

"*Love?*" Mang Andres said, his head snapping up to glare at the *kapre* above him. "Do not delude yourself! She was merely good to you, just as she was to everyone else! She never loved you, how could she love a monster like you?"

"Unfortunately," Juan said quietly, "She did."

Mang Andres stared at him, mouth open.

"Help me out a bit here, Maria," Juan said. "What are the two things that make a *kapre* different from all the other *enkantos*?"

"The fact that they live in trees, I suppose," Maria said, looking not at all pleased, "and the cigars they smoke; the smell is really quite horrendous."

"Exactly." He brought out the piece of cloth from his pockets, and handed it to Mang Andres. "Smell it. You too, Maria."

"It smells of cigar smoke," the Lady Sinukuan said, immediately turning away and covering her nose with a handkerchief from her pocket.

"And I got this from the *Señorita* Victoria's bedsheets," Juan said. "It's a smell distinct to the cigar of a *kapre*. It really is quite hard to wash off, even with repeated soaking. So what would this smell be doing in a lady's bed then, if all the lady gave the *kapre* were smiles and nice words?"

The *kapre* jumped down from the mango tree, making the ground rumble. "I loved her, that is true," he said to the now white-faced Mang Andres, "and she loved me. But I told her that we could never be. I was not human like her, or mortal. So she consented to marry that boy, Florante."

"But why refuse to cut down your tree?" Mang Andres said. "There are many trees here, and in the forest. You could easily move away and leave us be!"

"Do you think it is that easy," the *kapre* said with blazing eyes, "to move into a new home? Just as you mortals need an entire year or two to build a house, we need some time as well! She only sought to delay you for a few more months, that was all she asked! She did not ask for your consent to love me, no. Don't you ever listen to your daughter?"

Mang Andres glared back at the *kapre*. "Answer me then— is it true that she refused to marry Florante because—"

"The very thought!" the *kapre* cried out. "She only wished to call off the wedding to give me time to prepare my new home. That is all!"

"You have always suspected that she loved this *kapre*," the Lady Sinukuan finally spoke. "I see the truth of this, as plainly as if I could see into your heart. Was that what you accused her of, the morning she called off the wedding? That she carried that *kapre's* child within her?"

He crumpled the piece of cloth he held in his hand. "I see my accusation was not entirely unfounded."

"Perhaps," the *kapre* said, "But it is impossible!"

"We'll never know now, in any case," Juan said. "What I *can* tell you, however, is how your daughter died."

The *kapre* did not say anything, and only hung his head, shaking all over. Mang Andres noticed this, and walked right up to the *kapre*, and spat in his face.

"You knew?" he shrieked. "You knew of her death? Then you were responsible!"

The kapre pushed him away, and cried out in a great voice,

dropping his cigar on the ground. "I only knew of her death because I felt it! But I did not kill her, why would I? I loved her! How could you kill someone you love?"

"That can happen though, by accident," Juan said. "Where were you the evening before?"

"I was away the whole morning," said the *kapre*, "and well into the evening. I was gathering materials for my new home in the Lady Sinukuan's forest . . . I hurried back as soon as I felt her death. When I got here, I found my tree nothing but mere ash, burned to the ground. And my beloved was dead . . ."

"Who believes your excuses?" Mang Andres said angrily. "You killed her, *kapre*. Aren't I right, Juan? He killed her, didn't he?"

"No, Mang Andres," Juan said quietly. "You did."

Mang Andres could only stare at him.

"Mang Andres, did you never wonder how *kapres* are able to live in trees?" Juan said. "It really would be uncomfortable to live among the branches, there's nothing to lie on, and one can so easily fall while sleeping and break one's neck."

There was still no answer, and Juan went on.

"A talent *enkantos* have," he said, "Is to create another realm where only they can go to, and there they really live. It is hard to explain, but imagine this: within the branches of that acacia tree is another unseen room, the *kapre's* realm, where none can enter except this *kapre*, and anyone else he permits to enter. The young lady, because you loved her, you allowed her to enter, am I right?" Juan said to the *kapre*. "And she could do so even without you having to be there with her?"

The *kapre* nodded. "She only has to climb the tree, and wish to be inside my realm . . ." He stopped, his eyes on Mang Andres, unblinking.

"There you have your answer," Juan said grimly.

"I'm afraid . . . I don't understand . . ." Mang Andres said.

Juan brought out the other contents of his pocket, and he showed them the burnt branch he obtained from beneath the acacia tree, and the flower petals. "This branch, undoubtedly, is from the acacia tree. This is what its flowers look like, look very closely. This flower, obviously, is not from the acacia."

"It's a gumamela, I think," the Lady Sinukuan observed.

"Yes," Juan said. "You like wearing these too, then?" He put the flower beneath her ear, and she slapped his hand away. "Very beautiful. No wonder young women these days like to wear it too. Victoria did, too, based on her portrait."

"She did," Mang Andres murmured. "But what does—"

"You still don't see?" Juan said incredulously. "When she left you the morning before, she ran away to the home of her beloved. She climbed up the acacia tree and entered his realm. He was not there, so she waited for him. But then you came in the evening and in anger burned the acacia—"

Mang Andres collapsed on his knees with a strangled cry.

"Burning her with it," Juan said. "She could not get out in time, for the whole tree was already burning by the time the flames reached the *kapre's* realm."

Mang Andres began to weep, more bitterly than he had done before, while the *kapre* leapt towards the stump of the acacia tree, and knelt before it.

"This is why your seekers could not find her," Juan said to Maria, "This is all that is left of her." He brought out another piece of cloth, where beneath its folds lay a small mound of ash. "Give this to him when he finally recovers from this piece of news, although I think no one can ever really recover from something like this. I'll return tomorrow, and then we can finally discuss our wedding plans."

A strong gust of wind suddenly threw him off his feet, and he landed inches away from the hem of the Lady Sinukuan's skirt.

"Who are you, really?" the Lady Sinukuan said, her voice low and dangerous. "What did you come here for?"

"To marry you," Juan said earnestly. "Really. I came here all the way here just to see you."

"That burn mark on your hand is shaped like the inscriptions on the amulet that the townspeople have, to protect them from the *enkantos*. Then you are—"

Juan smiled. "You *are* perceptive. I really mean no harm. Many people are like Mang Andres, who fear *enkantos*, without any reason. I only wished to prove that humans are just as capable of things that can strike terror into the hearts of many. And I think that with our marriage, people will finally see differently . . ."

"I will never marry you," she declared.

"I am offended that you would not think to marry me just because of what I am," Juan said. "Someday you'll think differently, and I will wait until you do."

The air around him crackled, and the Lady Sinukuan's eyes glowed once more.

"At least you should thank me for helping you," Juan said, pouting. "But it's all right, I love you, and love forgives everything. Until tomorrow, then, dear Maria."

He galloped away, managing to escape the hail of rocks that she sent his way.

"I suppose I do have to thank you," the Lady Sinukuan said, looking first at the weeping man behind her and the *kapre* by the acacia tree, "but that doesn't change anything."

She shaded her eyes from the light of the morning sun. She strained to see into the distance, but only saw the silhouette of a horse, standing on its two rear legs. It nodded as if it heard her. There came a distant whinnying, and the creature melted away into nothingness, becoming one with the shadows beneath the trees.

MELU

Offerings to Aman Sinaya

Andrei Tupaz

Andrei Tupaz completed a creative writing degree in 2005, worked as an English teacher for three years, and now works in the IT industry. He spends his free time reading (anything that strikes his fancy), signing up for online courses that interest him, and on rare occasions, writing stories. He and his wife live in New Zealand.

Since the Philippines is an archipelago, it's easy to understand why the deities of the sea would be so important. Aman Sinaya was the Tagalog goddess of the sea, and protector of fishermen . . . protector, that is, for as long as the fishermen would offer to her their first catch. But as times change, so too does the nature of what is offered.

Once every three years, during what is called an offering year, the chosen and his wife sail south, away from their home island of Kaybulan. They go past the central islands, skirting both natural and man-made obstructions, never landing on shore, sailing always toward what they know is the gateway to Aman Sinaya's domain—a disc of placid seawater, situated between the central and southern islands.

Not everyone can find the gateway. Only those who have read the waves, the currents, the wind, and the night sky since they were children, and who can dream that waveless waters exist in the midst of windy seas, can ever be in her presence. And those who still give homage to the sea goddess Aman Sinaya know that she will hide herself if one's desire to find her is weak.

It is desire too—the desire to express one's life to the goddess—that helps a chosen pick the purest offering. The offerings which Aman Sinaya considers are mementos imbued with strong echoes of human emotions. A child's first fallen tooth, a hat of *binakol* fabric that a woman wove for her husband, or the hook used by a line fisherman for his first big catch—all these can be worthy offerings, but only if their original owners wish for Aman Sinaya to have them.

Tadyo's desire to see Aman Sinaya has never been weak. Eighteen years ago, when Tadyo turned twelve he borrowed his father's boat, brought his purest offering, and sailed south, to search for Aman Sinaya. He found the gateway to the sea goddess's domain, and tried breaching it, but did not have the strength. He returned to his tribe, dejected.

When he reached the southern shore of his home island he saw his father and Afif, the chosen of their tribe, standing by the shore, waiting for him.

"Aman Sinaya favors you. She admires your strength, and your belief in the old ways," Afif said.

But I failed, Tadyo said. I was not able to see her.

"The times when a man could see through a pure offering and will alone are gone," Afif said. "Now, only the chosen are allowed near her presence." Afif paused, gazed at Tadyo's face, and then said, "I have already notified the elders."

And with those words, Afif walked back to the forest. Tadyo and his father went straight to the hut of the tribal elders.

The elders were worried because Afif had become remiss in his duties. For the past six years, Afif had withdrawn from tribal gatherings. He had even built a hut in the middle of their island's forest, so that no one could bother him and his wife.

It was the chosen's duty to bless the fishermen and the boats, and to point the fishermen to fertile waters. None of this did Afif do anymore. The only ritual Afif still adhered to was the offering ritual.

So now each season's catch is weak, some of the elders said. Now our younger ones have no choice but to leave our tribe, and find work in the city. Now they work as house servants, or dive for coins for the amusement of tourists, or work as fishermen for large fishing vessels.

The elders who still believed in Afif said: Afif has done his job. For forty years he did his job. But he is too old now. He needs his rest.

All the elders agreed: they would not bother Afif anymore. They understood he was tired. Tadyo had to replace Afif.

No one became chosen without being married first. Thus, Tadyo had to marry.

But by then very few of the tribe's mothers wanted their daughters married to someone marked by Aman Sinaya. The elders could decree all they want, but they knew what they wanted. Only one mother in the whole tribe did not mind her daughter marrying Tadyo. In fact, she encouraged it. This woman was their neighbor Manang Luz, a woman who had been abandoned by her husband.

Some of the women whispered amongst themselves: But really, did you expect a woman who is rarely here to watch out for her daughter's welfare?

The women were referring to the fact that Manang Luz left Kaybulan once each week, on Friday, to visit one of the provinces in the western islands. Supposedly she had a business, selling stocks of bottled fish. The members of the tribe didn't believe this, of course. They knew she had a lover there. Whenever Manang Luz left, she'd ask Tadyo's parents to take care of Adara, her only child. Tadyo's parents always agreed to Manang Luz's weekly request.

So it was that by the age of eight Tadyo became used to having Adara in his house. Every time Manang Luz returned to pick up her daughter, she looked for Tadyo first. For wherever Tadyo was, there she knew her daughter was also.

If she returned to Kaybulan in the morning, Manang Luz would trek to the northern beach. There she'd find Tadyo and Adara immersed waist-deep in water, trying, but always failing, to catch anchovies with their hands. In the afternoons, she knew the children played at the edge of the forest, near the beach. Running from tree to tree, they'd say they were hunting for tree spirits. At night, the two children would be at the home of Tadyo's parents. They'd be sitting cross-legged in one corner of the hut, looking at, what seemed to be random objects—a twig, a piece of rope, bottled water. When she arrived, they'd turn around, trying to hide the objects. Sometimes Manang Luz would pause before she entered the hut, and hear the two children talking about the objects. Isn't the twig more important than the rope? What about the bottled water?

Sometimes Manang Luz greeted the two children by saying, "Ah, here's the married couple."

While Adara chided her mother, Tadyo would blush and frown. Manang Luz, seeing the blush on Tadyo's cheeks, would smile.

After the elders told Tadyo to get married, Manang Luz thought long and hard about her status in Kaybulan. She knew her neighbors whispered about her. She knew they blamed her for something that had never been her fault.

She came to one conclusion: her visibility in Kaybulan affected Adara negatively.

Manang Luz made her decision. She informed Tadyo's parents that her business was starting to become more profitable. Hence, she needed to stay in the western islands more days out of a week. Could you take care of my daughter, please?

Of course, Tadyo's parents said. Of course.

By then, many things had changed for Tadyo. He spent most of his time at sea, learning the ways of fishermen from his father. At night, under the stars, his father told him again and again their tribe's stories of creation: how the first man and woman were made. How the first man and woman found the forests inhospitable, full of warring spirits, so they turned to the waters around them. There, they found, only Aman Sinaya reigned. They asked Aman Sinaya if they could take from her domain, and the sea goddess gazed at them with all her power and said: "Explain to me why."

These stories his father had told him ever since he was a toddler. And now, hearing them after he had been marked by Aman Sinaya, he felt a sense of place. He felt the purpose behind the path he had taken.

After dawn they'd return with their catch to their house near the shore. His mother was there, as was Adara, who had become his mother's helper. Adara was learning what a wife's work was all about. It was unnerving to see his former playmate apprenticed to his mother, preparing food, helping his mother with the cooking, and always with a focused, attentive look that she never had when they played their games.

It unnerved him even more when he'd start talking to Adara, and notice, from the corner of his eyes, that his parents were observing the way he and Adara interacted with each other.

The day Tadyo turned fifteen, he and Adara were wed, on the southern shores of Kaybulan. As was custom, Afif, the retiring chosen, attended the wedding so he could formally pass on his duties to Tadyo. But Afif did not follow tribal traditions. Instead of performing the ritual of Succession in public, Afif said he'd talk to Tadyo and Adara privately. The tribe's elders whispered amongst themselves.

Afif seemed not to notice the elder's whispers. He stood up, told the newlyweds to follow him, and walked away from the gathering, toward the north. Tadyo and Adara followed.

They stopped at the northern beach. Afif walked towards the water until he was waist-deep. "Come," he said.

The two teenagers joined him.

He told the newlyweds to stand beside each other, his right shoulder touching her left. After they had done so, he told them to immerse their hands underwater, side by side, their hands touching, to form a large cup.

They did so, and an anchovy swam into the one cup that both their hands had formed.

Adara gasped in wonder. This was the power of the chosen, she realized.

Another anchovy swam into their hands, and then two, and suddenly the cup they had formed with their hands was being filled with anchovies that had swum in; so many anchovies wriggling, fighting to get into their cupped hands, stacking on one top of each other. Adara gasped again, this time in fright. She snatched her hand back, and the cup they had formed was broken, and the anchovies swam away.

Afif looked directly at Adara and said: "The elders think Tadyo must marry because there has never been an unmarried chosen. They think your marriage is purely a matter of tradition. They are wrong. Tadyo is chosen because you are with him. If you leave, he will cease to be chosen. Alone, he does not have the strength to see her. He will never be able to draw from her well."

And Afif started walking away from them, towards the clearing in front of the newlyweds. When he reached the clearing, he extended his hand forward. A shadow moved from behind one of the bushes. A hand reached out to grasp Afif's hand.

"Let's go home," the newlyweds heard the shadow say, in a woman's voice, clear and light.

Afif nodded his head, and stepped into the shadows.

The newlyweds stood there. Adara wished it was morning, so she could stare at the face of Afif's wife Maria. For the last time anyone had seen Maria had been during the last offering year, two years ago.

But all that has passed.

Our marriage was fifteen years ago, and the world is now barely the same, Tadyo thinks, as he sits on the boat, and stares at the sky. Yet we're still here.

Adara, sitting beside him, pokes him in the shoulder, and with a smile, says. "Shouldn't we start?"

"Yes, we should," he says.

The full moon has already reached its apex in the sky, and with its light it exposes Aman's Sinaya's silent waters to them. There, thirty meters from their boat's portside, is a part of the sea that's so calm its surface has turned into a perfect mirror, reflecting the moon and the constellations in the sky.

Before they begin, Tadyo takes down the already-furled mast, and lays it on the hull of the boat. Adara, leaning starboard, washes her hands in the seawater, and then walks to the fore of their boat. Under the seat, there is a large icebox which she takes out, and opens. Inside, among the nylon tackle lines, hooks, and can of bait, are two folded blankets. One is white. The other was once white, but now has a topmost fold stained with dried blood. Looking at the blood stains in the moonlight, she shudders for a second.

Adara wants to tell her husband to pick another offering, something she thinks is more worthy. But she doesn't. Instead, she walks to where her husband is, unfolds the blanket, and wraps it around his waist twice. Tadyo smiles at her.

"I'll tie it myself," he says.

Adara nods, walks back to the icebox. She closes the icebox but doesn't return it to its storage place underneath the front seat. Instead she puts it in the center of the *bangka*. Then she turns to the stern of the boat.

She dives cleanly, the boat bobbing once at her departure. Tadyo follows.

Tadyo and adara float on their backs with their hands linked, their faces mostly immersed. Only their noses and mouths break the water's surface. The breeze, which is gentle, blows across the water but doesn't disturb it. The breeze is a bit colder than the water. The two would welcome it if they could feel it. They're trying to immerse themselves in the cold. They're trying to slow their hearts down.

Tadyo squeezes his wife's hands. They take deep rapid breaths, expelling and inhaling as much air as they can. Ten breaths, and then Tadyo squeezes his wife's hand again, and when she squeezes back, he releases her hand. They dive into the water at the same time.

In the darkness, their leg and arm strokes are long, languid ones. After five strokes they stop, and reach for each other again. Their bodies are relaxed but straight. The water claims them, and pulls them down. Schools of shadows flit about them; sea life they can't see brush against their bodies. But no animals dare harm them. Not the chosen, not in Aman Sinaya's domain.

Faint lights blink through the darkness, like stars in the night sky. Tadyo and Adara admire the lights for a second, then close their eyes. There are stories of those seeking Aman Sinaya who, intrigued by the lights, veered away from the proper path, and become lost, their bodies crushed, their spirits absorbed by sea creatures.

There is only one path, straight down, into pure darkness, while above them whatever is left of the moon's light disappears. Tadyo sometimes feels he is not swimming down but flying up, towards the darkest part of the heavens.

A current envelops them. When it ends, all the faint lights in the distance have disappeared. There is a new light directly below them now, a disc of green light, like a green moon.

Adara reaches for Tadyo. She hugs him. She presses her lips against his lips. Tadyo exhales old air through his nose, and then opens his mouth, to receive his wife's breath. Her breath fills his lungs anew.

Tadyo releases his wife. Once he is clear of her, she flips right-side up, and begins to move upward, towards the surface. After she passes the current, she reminds herself to use more efficient strokes. Wasted movements might mean a blackout.

Tadyo's almost at her domain.

The disc of light is a coral reef a hundred meters in diameter, shaped into a perfect circle, glowing with fluorescent light. At the center of the reef stands her grotto—Aman Sinaya's domain, the heart of her underwater garden.

Things have changed, he knows. He doesn't want to think of the changes for now. For now, he wants to enjoy the feel of being in this holy place again, as the water pulls him down.

An arm's length away from the grotto, he reaches out with both hands. He smiles at the feel of the barnacles in his hands. He pushes himself downward. He flips around, his feet landing softly on the seabed.

Inside the grotto is Aman Sinaya's aspect—a statue of a woman wearing a robe, her hair hidden by a headscarf. The statue's arms are extended in front of her. Her hands are cupped together. Her eyes are sad. The mouth is partially open. There's a pleading expression on her face, as if whatever Tadyo is going to give her will save her.

He has never shirked in his duties, Tadyo thinks.

Every day he blesses fishermen before they set off. Afterward, he takes off all his clothes, and submerges himself in the waters of the southern shores. He'll sit on the seabed and pray to Aman Sinaya. And when he emerges, he'll know whether the fishermen will get a good catch or not.

Once a week it's their boats he blesses, slitting his own wrist, and spilling his blood onto the hull of each boat, so that the waves and currents can sense his blood on the wood, and hopefully grant each boat safe passage. There was a time when all he had to do was submerge his wounded wrist, and the saltwater would heal it instantly. But nowadays, he prefers not using the sea's power.

And yet for all his adherence to the rituals, Aman Sinaya has never given more than an adequate catch. The older fishermen still speak of the last large haul—eight boats full of fish, and everyone in the tribe past the age of eight had to stop whatever they were doing to salt and preserve fish for the rainy season, and still two boats, almost drowning in fish, had to go to the city and sell their fish there, because there was too much, ay, just too much—knowing that those times are long gone, withered away, just as Afif and Maria withered and became old.

Some of the elders blame Afif, for Afif had only taught Tadyo for a week. It was as if Afif had not wanted Tadyo to succeed, those elders say. None of them understand that the chosen's rituals come from visions and dreams. Afif had told Tadyo early on: "These rituals we do to help the tribe are the tribe's rituals, not Aman Sinaya's rituals. They change with each chosen, as Aman's Sinaya's name, and the face she shows you changes. In the Eastern Isles she is called Maryam, Star of the sea. In the middle provinces, they call her Magwayen. Even the stories they tell of her vary from tribe to tribe. Only one ritual is constant—the offering. Adhere to the offering, and you'll hear her voice, and feel her power."

The younger fishermen look at Tadyo's actions, and dismiss their efficacy. The powers of the chosen are an old belief, just another harmless and quaint superstition their fathers and the older fishermen cling to.

Nowadays, what occupies the minds of the younger fishermen are the motorized boats that visit their fishing grounds, from the purse-seiners that encircle tuna, to the trawlers that take, in a day's catch, what could feed their tribe for months. Every time one appears, they know they'll be lucky if they catch anything.

Once, all the fishermen spotted a dilapidated boat full of children, and only three adults. The boat stopped at the western side of their island, and all the children dove into the sea. After the boat left, it was like the corals had been pounded clean. The western side of their island is, till now, an underwater desert.

They hear stories that foreign fishing vessels, containing as much as a hundred men, sometimes visit their waters.

Sometimes, Tadyo hears the younger fishermen speculating on the future. If this keeps up, the young ones sometimes say, we'll all end up working in the city, on the same boats that steal our fish.

Adara is already at the surface. She floats on her back, and looks at the moon.

She remembers the first time they did this ritual. The first time she saw the light of Aman Sinaya's domain in the distance, the first time she gave him her breath, she had kissed him—a true kiss, not just a touching of lips. He had kissed her back, cupping her head tenderly in his arms before letting her go.

She remembers she had not gone up at once, but had actually paused for a few seconds, and admired the light of Aman Sinaya in the distance, in the same way she now admires the moon. She had made a vow, that she would always kiss him when she shared her breath with him. For who else could say they had kissed, with the light of the most holy of places shining in the distance?

At aman Sinaya's domain, Tadyo notices some corals are losing their light, and turning black. There was a time when he'd be greeted by sea life swimming all around her garden: angel fish, parrot fish, butterfly fish, clownfish, seahorses and snappers. Up until two offering rituals ago, there were still some seahorses, but now there's no life aside from these corals, the barnacles covering her grotto, and the seaweed which, he notices, have also lessened.

He walks towards her aspect, her idol. This, he knows, is the closest he'd ever get to seeing Aman Sinaya's true face. And even this he knows is just a facet, one chosen specially for him. As Afif used to say, each chosen sees a different face.

He bows in front of her, kneels, kisses both her feet and prays silently, in the manner of their tribe. Then, he unties the blanket at his waist. He stands up, wraps the blanket around her cupped hands, ties it. He kneels again, and kisses both her feet a second time. This time his kiss lingers. He stands up, starts stepping back, always keeping her aspect in his eyes. The moment he clears the grotto, he begins swimming up.

He can feel Aman Sinaya's spirit in him now.

Next time he visits he knows the blanket will be gone, torn into minuscule pieces by the sea, absorbed by Aman Sinaya.

It is, and always has been, his grace and flaw, he thinks, to hearken to his father's stories, and be enamored by them. For if he did not need to believe in his father's stories, or in the tribe's rituals, he would not have begun gathering mementos, and looking at them each night—like the seashell he plucked from the seabed during his first thirty-feet freedive, or the piece of the sailing rope that had burned his hands the first time he tried sailing his father's boat alone, or the mast that he took from the remains of Afif's boat, the day after he buried Afif and his wife. He would not have dragged Adara into his obsession. Adara would not have added the twig, taken from a banana tree, in the forest where they used to play, or the water she had taken from the northern beach, or the baby bottle which she had bought prematurely.

Each night Tadyo and his wife look at the mementos they have gathered. Each night they ask themselves: Which memento is worthy? Which memento will make the sea goddess understand?

Adara swims, waiting for her husband to emerge. Her mind flits from thought to thought. She remembers when they left the southern shores, there were four young fishermen sitting on the beach, swigging coconut wine while complaining about the weakening catch.

I wonder what they'd say if they saw what we've seen on our journeys, she thinks. She closes her eyes, remembering some of it.

In the midst of the ocean, the waves, the constellations in

the sky and the sealife flowing below their boat, pockets of disruption. Large steel and iron fishing vessels, some of them rusty, scooping up, encircling or attracting fish. Flashy light-filled tourist vessels moving through the night, their human noise transmitting through the waters they displace. At the western isles we took a break, and saw in the distance a steel tower rising out of the ocean. There's a seaside mining plant on the central coast where fish dare not swim. At the southernmost island of the central coast, seabirds choke on crude oil.

Adara grabs her husband just as he reaches the surface. She spins behind him, then wedges her forearms under his armpits so that she can hoist him up, and rest his head on her chest. He's gasping almost instinctively, his whole body shaking.

She swims on her back, toward the boat, using mostly her legs because she must hold onto her husband, must try to keep his head, that is shaking so violently, stable on her chest, must try to keep his head facing up toward the moon, so he doesn't ingest any water. She turns her head back from time to time to ensure she's facing the right direction. Hold on please, she thinks. Just until we've reached our boat.

Somehow Tadyo finds the strength to pull himself up the boat. He flops onto the hull, collapses. Adara follows. In a split second, she's climbed up, opened the icebox, grabbed the blanket and has wrapped it around her husband.

The first three times they did the Offering ritual, Tadyo would kiss Aman Sinaya's feet, and then surface, filled with her gift, a calmness of mind and knowledge of the water that allowed him to feel the heartbeat of a whale shark a hundred miles away, see the migration paths of fish the moment he looked at the waves, and know which schools of fish swimming in an area were mature, ready to be caught. He'd surface, kiss his wife passionately, thus sharing the sea goddess's power with her, and they'd smile. Though the air was colder than it was now, they never felt cold, for their veins flowed with life.

But now, the gift that courses through Tadyo's veins is tainted with poison. In his mind, Tadyo hears an unrelenting echo of a scream. His arms and legs are numb. His lungs and belly are on fire. His vision: disappearing.

It is only when his wife kisses him that the darkness and the screaming begin to recede. He returns her kiss, cupping her head in his trembling arms.

Later when he is strong enough, Tadyo hugs his wife, sharing the blanket with her. She is crying in pain, mewling like a baby.

He makes sure the blanket covers both of them completely. This time, just like the last time, her tears drip onto the blanket, staining it red.

PATAG'AES

Balat, Buwan, Ngalan
(A Myth for the 21ˢᵗ Century)

David Hontiveros

*David Hontiveros was a 1997 National Book Award Final-
ist in the Best Comic Book category for "Dhampyr" (drawn by
Oliver Pulumbarit), and a 2002 Palanca Award Winner (2nd
Place in the Future Fiction- English Category) for his short story, "Kaming Mga Seroks." He has three horror/dark fantasy no-
vellas out under the Penumbra imprint, published by Visprint,
as well as a digital novel, "Pelicula", from Bronze Age Media.
His on-going comic book series, "Bathala: Apokalypsis", is also
available digitally from Flipside. He has had his short fiction,
film reviews, articles, and comics appear in several Philippine
publications. He has adapted Bret Harte (no, not the wrestler)
and Edgar Allan Poe (twice!) into comic book form for Graphic Classics. He may be observed online at fiveleggediguana.
blogspot.com (where he blathers on about film) and david-
hontiveros.com (where assorted bits of his work are housed).
He would like to humbly dedicate the story to his four current
grandspawn, in chronological order: Gray, Mischa, Chloe, and
Sophia, who will keep the flames of his family history burning
on, down through the years.*

*While the Philippines is home to distinct cultural groups, a cer-
tain amount of cultural cross-pollination did take place. The
results are myths which are variations of the same themes, and
characters which appear in more than one culture, or who bear
the same name but with an altered form. But, as David says of*

this story: there is power in words and there is truth in myth.
If these characters did exist . . . which version would be true?
Would it matter?

i.

You enter the club, a nameless little hole-in-the-wall just off Timog, into the electric blue nicotine haze and white hot stutter-strobe. At the far end of the narrow interior, on the tiny stage, a band of PDBs play, a cover of "Marian" so funereal, it would make Andrew Eldritch contemplate open over doors and pearl-handled razors.

The lead singer, Jim Morrison-shirtless, feet Doc Martens-clad, tattered and stained taffeta skirt worn over tight leather pants, croons into the microphone in a vaguely intimate manner, the deep, graveyard sound of his voice issuing from lips gleaming with a color identified on an exclusive online catalogue as "Bruise Pristine."

The singer looks at you with piercing, mascaraed eyes, and a shiver crawls up your spine, disembodied hand from *Macabra*, going for your neck.

You rip your gaze away from him and search the crowd, all tribal-tattooed and pierced, enough stray bits in this place to set the NAIA metal detectors keening like grieving banshees.

There. You see him. (Though you know this is merely because he *allows* himself to be seen. Otherwise, there would seem to be nothing but an empty chair.) Short, fat, bearded and long-haired, he looks like Gimli. (You forget the actor's name just now. John something-something. The guy who played Indy's sidekick.)

He looks bored and irritable, the little man, the *karibang* in the walking shorts, rubber slippers, and *Species* t-shirt: Natasha Henstridge in mid-morph, slowly turning into the H.R. Giger monstrosity with the killer nipples.

His back pointedly turned to the stage, he sees you, and frowns, his bushy werewolf eyebrows meeting over the bridge of his plump, overripe tomato nose. He gestures impatiently with one hand, and you hurry to his table, taking the seat opposite him.

He grumbles something under his breath, something that sounds like "Damn demon onion," and you're uncertain what he's referring to (or even that you heard right), and are about to ask him, when he leans forward and says, "Show me."

You reach into your backpack and pull out a Ri-Data CD in a clear plastic slimline case, putting it on the table.

"DivX," you say.

"Subtitles?" he asks, a challenge almost.

"Sorry. It's raw."

The werewolf eyebrows meet, tussle, then he expels an irritated sigh. "It's okay. How much talking can she do if all she does is run? Anyway, had a kobold girlfriend once."

"I've got *Try Seventeen* on DVD," you offer casually.

The *karibang* sneers. "Mandy Moore," he says, turning the name into an epithet.

"She's hardly there," you assure him.

He shakes his head, Gimli locks whipping about violently. "Get me *Anatomie*."

"I'll try," you say non-commitally, recalling what a let-down that film had been.

"Marian" segues neatly into "Black Planet," and the *karibang* groans, rolling his eyes.

"So," you say.

He nods once, then begins to speak.

"Daga had already become the earth, just as his siblings were already the sun, the seven moons, and the numberless stars.

"And just as heaven and hell had seven layers each, so did the earth—when it formed from Daga's body of rock—have seven layers of its own.

"This layer, upon which we reside at the moment, is the first, uppermost layer. The second, below us, the deep places of the world where my kind live. And below our caverns, still other layers, and other peoples.

"On the uppermost layer though, *this* layer," waving his stubby-fingered hand to encompass the club and its customers, "Magbabaya was having problems with," closing his hand into a fist, then lifting his forefinger, "the waters of chaos, what the Egyptians called Nun, and," lifting his middle finger, "Bakunawa, the huge, torturous serpent that rules the seas, the beast with seven frightful heads and gleaming, green eyes, the terrible mad dragon of old, known by other names: Lotan in the Ras Shamra texts, Livyatan to the Jews, Leviathan in the Bible."

He puts down his hand, on the table, fingers just touching the edge of the CD case.

"Magbabaya needed to put Bakunawa in his place, for the piercing and crooked serpent had been up to mischief, swallowing moon after moon—another tale, for another time—till there was just the one left, and the Creator knew he had to put a stop to the mad dragon's hunger. So he slew the serpent—for which we *karibang* will always be grateful to Magbabaya, as Bakunawa had been using our caverns as a lair, fouling them with droppings and the reek of his sulfurous breath—and took the sprawling expanse of the thick, scaly skin, to form a firmament, the *raqia*, which separated the celestial waters from the terrestrial, creating a space upon which life could proliferate, and holding back the waters of chaos, where they roiled, above.

"But there was still a little of the serpent's skin left over after this, and, understanding that Bakunawa still had a role to play in this drama, Magbabaya formed a new Bakunawa far smaller than the huge, torturous serpent only recently slain, and let this newly-birthed Bakunawa roam the wide and dry lands of the earth.

"And still, there was a tiny portion of the skin unused, so Magbabaya put this aside, for he was beginning to have an idea for the creatures who would live on this new, dry land, and wished to use this skin to clothe these as-yet unmade creatures, whom he had decided to call 'men.'

"Meanwhile, the shadow of the great dragon, living on past its death, continued to soar the skies, still enraptured of the last moon and its silver light, re-enacting that final attempt to swallow it, as a ghost would, over and over and over again."

And you know the tale is at its end, as the *karibang's* hand moves onto the CD case, then slides it across the table, towards him.

You blink, and suddenly, he is no longer at the table. All there is across from you now is an empty chair.

On the stage, the band shifts Goth gears and launches into The Mission's "Wasteland," and you remember: John Rhys-Davies.

You nod to yourself, stand, and walk to the door, trying to recall where you'd tucked that VHS tape of *Anatomie* away.

ii.

Though you are relatively anal in certain aspects of your life, you do wish you were a little more organized. Converting *Anatomie* from its VHS format and burning the film onto a DVD had been easy; finding the tape had taken the better part of a week.

It would have been far easier to just Google an *Anatomie* torrent, but you're dealing with a *karibang*, and there are certain rules, so the gift to be exchanged cannot be procured nor purchased solely for that purpose; it must be something already previously owned. Thus, the week-long search for the elusive, Sasquatch-like, VHS tape. (It had been in a Nicoli cereal box—repurposed as a containment unit for VHS tapes—at the back of one of your closet's shelves, together with your copies of *Santa Sangre* and *The Reflecting Skin*, the last with a young and still unknown Viggo Mortensen.)

And now, here you are, in a posh coffee place in Greenbelt, and you've actually paid more than the cost of a decent lunch, in return for coffee that tastes . . . okay. You hate these kinds of exorbitantly-priced places. Every time you're in one of them, you have the irrational urge to shout "Operation Latte Thunder!" at the top of your lungs, and pump your fist militantly in the air.

So when the little man just appears in the chair across from you, between one eye blink to the next, you heave a sigh of relief. He is dressed to blend in now, long-sleeved polo shirt, slacks, patent leather shoes.

His latte is in front of him, and he looks almost eager. You imagine his short legs swinging, child-like, below the table.

Wordlessly, you pass the slimline-cased DVD across the table, and the *karibang* takes a deep lungful of latte steam through his nostrils.

Eyes closed, he smiles, looking about as content as you've ever seen him.

Then, he opens his eyes, looks at you, and begins to speak.

"Bakunawa's great love was the beautiful Bulan, who found, past the fearsome visage, a heart she could pledge her undying loyalty and love to.

"But due to the arrogance and ambition of Bulan's brother,

Daga, the love she shared with Bakunawa was to be rent asunder through no fault of their own. An attempt to storm the gates of heaven ended in divine retribution: Punished, along with Daga and her two other brothers, Bulan was struck by lightning sent down by Magbabaya from the seventh heaven, shattering her body into seven pieces.

"However, regretting the rashness with which he reacted to Daga's actions, the Creator blessed Bulan and her two other brothers, granting divine light upon the objects they had been turned into by his lightning.

"And thus did her brother Bitoon become the numberless stars, her other brother Adlao, the sun, and she, the seven moons.

"Daga, arrogant instigator, was given no light of his own, and became the earth upon which we live.

"Bakunawa, meanwhile, mourned the passing of his beloved Bulan, and it was from that deep, fathomless grief, that his hatred for Magbabaya stemmed.

"Night after night, the huge serpent Bakunawa stared longingly up at the seven moons, all that was left of his beloved, imagining the lap of water against his scales as her hands, soft and tender. From his lair in the second layer of the earth, in the caverns my people call home, Bakunawa would slither up, onto the first layer of the earth, still covered by the waters of chaos, and look upon Bulan, and dream of the warm, loving past, and the cold, bleak future.

"Finally, one evening, when his hunger and his grief and his pain were simply too much to bear, Bakunawa flew upwards, into the sky, and opened his jaws wide, wide, and wider still, till he could swallow one of the moons whole, which he did, and plunged back into the churning waters of chaos, to return to his lair.

"And there, he stayed for a month, part of Bulan within

him, and he could feel her, hear her thoughts, recall the love they had felt for one another, and it seemed that her hands, soft and tender, were *inside* him now, and for a time, Bakunawa knew happiness once more.

"But the month passed, and Bakunawa could feel that part of Bulan that was the moon he had swallowed, melt and wane within him, and the warm memories went with her, dissolving, her silvery light dying, and the grief came flooding back, and the great dragon began to choke on the bile of bitter remembrance.

"So again, Bakunawa emerged from the dark caves and flew into the sky and opened his jaws wide, wide, and wider still, and swallowed another moon whole.

"And the cycle began anew, only to end a month later, in hunger, and grief, and pain.

"Four more times he would do this, and four more months passed, and still, the void within him would inevitably return. And as those same months passed, Magbabaya took notice of the moons disappearing from the sky. Finally, when there was only the one left, the Creator asked my kind to be vigilant, and guard the last moon, for we were the people who lived closest to the surface, as man had yet to be made.

"Thus it was that when Bakunawa emerged from his lair that seventh time, we were there to see as he rose, gargantuan, into the night sky; there to see as his jaws opened wide, wide, and wider still; there to see him try to swallow the last moon, and thus, plunge the world into darkness.

"We beat on drums and howled as loudly as we could, shouting, '*Buhi-i ang among hampangan!*' and so great was the noise we *karibang* made that it did two things. The first, frighten the huge, torturous serpent before he could swallow the moon, sending him back to his lair in hunger and grief. The second, wake Magbabaya in time for him to see the very tip of

Bakunawa's long, winding tail splash into the waters of chaos.

"Thus comprehending the nature of the threat which the last moon faced, Magbabaya planted a bamboo tree on the moon—which can be seen as a dark spot on the face of the moon, sometimes mistaken for a rabbit, or a man—and so long as this bamboo tree is not chopped down, nothing can ever swallow the moon without also choking itself.

"Magbabaya then went on to slay the great dragon, so it could cause no more mischief. Still, Bakunawa's shadow tries, every now and then, to swallow the moon, causing what men know today as 'eclipses.' But the peoples of the earth who were told this story by my kind, know what to do.

"Though the Bagobo think Bakunawa's shadow is a great bird called *minokawa*; the Maranao, a huge lion called Arima-onga; the Manobo, a vast tarantula; and other peoples think him some other huge and terrible beast, they all know to make as much noise as they are able, and always, the noise frightens Bakunawa's shadow away, leaving the last part of his great love forever separate from him, all that is left in him—the shadow of the terrible mad dragon of old—is hunger, and grief, and pain."

You blink, as if awakening, and the *karibang* takes a small, almost dainty sip from his latte, enjoying it immensely.

You reach down, to the open backpack between your feet, and place another disc on the table.

The tips of the karibang's werewolf eyebrows collide. "What's that?" he asks suspiciously.

"*Der die Tollkirsche ausgräbt.*"

His eyes go wide, the breath catching in his chest.

"I only asked for *Anatomie*," he says, his eyes riveted to the CD.

"It's a freebie," you say, meaning it.

The *karibang* frowns, and you can feel the suspicion thicken, taste it as it curdles in the air.

"I'll take it," he says gruffly, already picking it up and placing it atop the *Anatomie* DVD, "but not as charity."

"It's not—"

"I'll pay for this," he says, and it's clear from his tone that there will be no argument. You stay silent, try to be as still as possible.

"I'll pay you," he continues, "but not now."

You nod, slowly.

"Now, I just want to enjoy my latte."

You stand, slinging your backpack over one shoulder. You hesitate, thinking to say something, but the little man has already turned all his attention to his latte. Once more, you nod to yourself, then walk away from the table, dreaming with your eyes wide open, of love, and of chaining one's self to the ghost of it, till the heart shrivels, and blows away on the gust of a desolate sigh.

iii.

You arrive at your apartment door at around half past nine, a blue plastic envelope tucked beneath your arm, freshly-printed reduced repros of a pair of one-sheets safe inside: Kim's *Janghwa, Hongryeon* and Balagueró's *Frágiles* (the official film poster, though you still prefer the teaser sheets). You're wondering where on your wall the glossy A4's are going, when you notice two things:

One, there's an unmarked brown envelope on the floor right in front of your apartment.

Two, something small (no more than two feet tall, certainly) and *black* peers at you from around the corner at the far end of the hall, with blank, white eyes, then twitters in some strange, chirping language, and skitters off towards the fire exit.

Shuddering, you reach down and pick the brown envelope up. Pressing lightly, you feel the interior lined with bubble pac, holding what you're guessing is an audio cassette.

Letting yourself into the small apartment you call "home," you place the plastic envelope on the chair by the door, before you lock up, and head to the futon in the room's corner.

You sit down, tearing a thin strip off the brown envelope's edge.

Shaking its contents into the palm of your hand, you see that it is, indeed, an audio tape, TDK SA-90, to be precise. Leaning forward, you slot the tape into the right deck of your Sony XO-D301 and press 'Play.'

At first, there is only the hiss of blank tape, then, the *karibang*'s voice, and all else—your hunger, the one-sheets—is forgotten.

All else, save the *karibang*'s words.

"Once, long ago, in a tiny village in Negros, very near to Mount Kanlaon, there lived a beautiful maiden, who was daughter to the village chief.

"She was fair and wondrous and virginal, all that is good and perfect in a young lady. All whom she blessed with her presence would feel touched somehow, as if by a higher power, and she was loved by her father beyond all else in the world.

"At the end of the festivities to celebrate the maiden's fourteenth birthday, the chief pronounced, 'No other man in our vast land is happier than I. I am blessed with peace, with a loving and obedient wife, and with a daughter whose beauty surpasses any in all of creation. There is nothing else I need or even desire.'

"No sooner had the last word left the chief's lips that a shadow fell upon him, embracing him in its darkness, though there was nothing which could be seen to cast the shadow at all. All who were witness to this, most especially his young daughter, shivered at the sight.

"The following morning, at the crack of dawn, as the raucous sound of roosters filled the air, three men were found, cold and dead, an odor most foul and fetid floating sluggishly on the winds.

"Even as the wails of mourning rose into the spreading dawn, many a villager caught sight of a great lumbering beast, which walked on two legs like a man, but had a vast head with five terrible faces, numerous green eyes, and a body thickly covered in scales. Flames belched from the beast's many nostrils, flames which emitted black smoke that stank and caused those who breathed it to fall ill.

"The thing lumbered back and forth, just beyond the village, blocking the path to the river, from whence the chief and his people took their water.

"At the sight of this menace, the chief came forward and addressed the beast, demanding to know its purpose.

"And the thing spoke, its voices a rumbling noise, like rolling thunder: 'I AM BAKUNAWA, AND I SHALL LEAVE YOUR PEOPLE BE, AND ALLOW THEM TO GATHER WATER FROM THE RIVER, IF YOU WOULD BUT GRANT ME A PLEASANT MEAL OF TWO CHICKENS A DAY.'

"Thus did the chief declare that a pair of chickens be granted to Bakunawa at the rising of each sun, so that his people be left in peace, for the lives of chickens were a far smaller price to pay than those of men.

"So did the days pass, and though Bakunawa left the villagers unharmed, they lived in fear, knowing the creature was watching, and that the chickens were lessening in number day by day.

"Finally, a group of the bravest of the village warriors spoke with the chief, asking him permission to slay Bakunawa, for they could not abide that their families and neighbors lived in constant terror of the cruel beast.

"'And what should happen, o chief,' the bravest of them asked, 'when there are no more chickens with which to feed Bakunawa's hunger?'

"And though the chief knew that he was sending these brave young men off to their doom, he nodded, a single tear falling from his eye.

"Thus did a dozen brave warriors do battle with Bakunawa, and that very day, a dozen brave warriors lost their lives, for the terrible, mad beast breathed flame and venomous fume upon them, tore into their soft, yielding flesh with his claws and fangs, while their spears and knives were unable to pierce the thick scales which covered Bakunawa like the hide of a crocodile.

"And no sooner had the last of the twelve braves fallen, lacking an arm and most of his neck, that Bakunawa roared: 'YOU DARE DEFY ME!'

"The chief looked out upon the grisly battlefield, the beast standing in a wet litter of innards, and knew defeat.

"'Humble apologies, mighty Bakunawa. Would you perhaps find pig to your liking?'

"And the thing grinned in a most hideous fashion, and raised its huge hands, and the chief saw that there, in its palms, were two more faces, and these faces spoke: 'By attacking me, little man, you spat on the words of honor used in our agreement. All I wanted was chicken, and you saw fit to deny me that. Now you offer me *pig*?'

"Then it spoke with all its seven terrible mouths.

"'A PLEASANT MEAL OF AN UNSPOILED MAIDEN A DAY, OR I SHALL BREATHE UPON YOUR DAMNABLE VILLAGE AND YOU SHALL ALL DIE MOST

WRETCHEDLY.'

"And with a heavy heart, while his people wailed and wept, the chief declared that Bakunawa would be fed an unspoiled maiden each dawn, a pair of tears falling from his eye.

"Thus, every dusk, a lottery was held, and the luckless child chosen would spend the last night with her parents, distraught and bereaved, then, bathed and perfumed and clad in black, would be given over to Bakunawa at first light.

"But as the days passed, and the sorrow and grief of the village became a thing one could taste, the chief's daughter noticed a strange thing.

"That morning, she stole to the clay jar which held the small pieces of wood for the lottery, the name of each young unmarried female carved, one to each. And she saw, to her horror, what her father the chief had done.

"She spent the rest of the morning in the deep woods, and returned just before noon, to the clay jar.

"That dusk, the chief reached into the jar, and, a jagged splinter digging deep into his thumb, pulled out a piece of freshly-carved wood, and shivered to see his daughter's name there.

"Amidst the gasps of the villagers, she walked, head held high, to her father's side, and in a voice only he could hear, whispered: 'My name and the names of the daughters of the village elders were never in that clay jar. You were letting the others suffer first, as if we are any better than they, for they have no titles nor honors, for they own less than we.'

"The chief looked into the jar, and saw his daughter's name carved into each and every piece of wood there. And when he looked up, his daughter turned away from him, and already feeling the sting of loss, shed three tears from his eye.

"The night, the chief's daughter spent with the villagers, as she did her best to comfort them in their grief. And if anyone noted that she did not seem to spend any time at all with her father, no one saw fit to say.

"As the few remaining roosters in the village greeted the rising sun, the chief's daughter, freshly-bathed, perfumed, and clad in a billowing black robe, strode away from the village, towards the waiting Bakunawa.

"Surely she would have suffered that day, had it not been for the arrival of the young warrior. Brave and handsome and strong of limb, this stranger was, and he wasted no time before he set upon Bakunawa and engaged him in vigorous combat.

"Though great and skilled were the blows the warrior struck against Bakunawa, a manner of combat the likes of which the village had never seen before, the creature's scales were proof against them. And as the battle raged, sparks and steam gushing and flying from the thing's mouths and nostrils, its poisonous breath soon began to take its toll on the youth, who staggered under the influence of the fumes.

"Bakunawa then caught the warrior in its thick arms, and with the strength of gargantuan pythons, began to crush the youth in its merciless grip.

"All seemed lost, the stranger pale and in pain, when suddenly, something white—like bone, like a shield, and yet like skin—seemed to burst forth from inside the youth's body, covering him from head to toe, and with ease, he broke free of Bakunawa's killing grasp.

"Now, it seemed as if the cruel beast was the one hard-pressed, for the warrior's blows were more powerful, and its breath no longer seemed to cause the youth any harm. Thus was Bakunawa finally felled by the mighty blows from the warrior's fists and feet, though the beast was not yet slain.

"The warrior turned to the chief's daughter, and asked for a long strip of black cloth from her robe, which she tore and handed to him, their fingers meeting, skin brushing against hard, white bone, or what she took to be bone, and the maiden shivered, masking her awe and delight.

"The warrior bound the strip of black cloth around Bakunawa's neck, and handed the other end of the cloth to the chief's daughter, that she might lead the beast to the very edge of the village.

"There, they were met by the chief and the village elders.

"The chief bowed deeply, and asked of the mighty warrior, 'What would you have as your reward, stranger, for saving my daughter and my village from the rampages of the cruel Bakunawa?'

"The warrior, still clad in the bone-white skin, replied in a voice deep and strong, '**I ask for nothing, save that Bakunawa's fate be decreed by your beautiful daughter.**'

"The chief's daughter looked first at the glowing blue eyes of the warrior, then at Bakunawa, the beast humbled, pitiful almost.

"Delicately, she untied the strip of black cloth from Bakunawa's neck.

"'Go. Leave with your life, but swear to never, ever, do again what you did here.'

"Bakunawa raised a single claw, and the face there spoke: 'I swear.'

"And the mad, terrible beast turned, and walked slowly away from the village, and if anyone noted the tears the maiden shed as she watched Bakunawa lumber away, no one saw fit to say.

"The warrior too, then turned and began to walk away, and would surely have left without another word, had not the maiden called out, 'To whom do I owe my life?'

"And the warrior stopped, and turned, and answered her."

You blink, the story at an end, and you are just about to

press 'Stop,' your stomach growling audibly, when the *karibang* speaks again, his tone different now, casual.

"So we're even for *Tollkirsche*. Do me this one favor though. Upload this story onto the 'net. Is that the right term? 'Upload'?

"I know you're putting all the stories I've told you into a book, and I wouldn't have told them to you otherwise, but I want this one out there, now. Get this out there for people to hear. These are the kinds of stories that shouldn't be forgotten.

"I know you know what I mean."

And you do.

coda

It has been precisely one year and a day since the night you uploaded the *karibang*'s last story to your blog. Shortly after, you began to sift through all of the myths and stories you had gathered for the book, the one you had always envisioned, the book that would collect and preserve all of these tales, once widespread and common, now rare and endangered.

The book, *Alamatia: Illuminating Modern-day Life Through Age-Old Legends*, has been out for a month now, and while sales are less than you'd hoped, they're steady as rain.

As part of the marketing push for *Alamatia*, you now find yourself at the latest geek convention, shrink-wrapped copies of your book stacked to the side, doing your best to keep pace with the modest line of people waiting for your signature.

Once the final person in line has been sent off gratefully (a young Goth girl-in-training, sporting a black *Coraline* t-shirt and purple highlights in her hair, who regarded your autograph as if it were both a sigil of blessing and a glyph of warding), you find yourself contemplating the sole copy of *Alamatia* at the table, the one meant for browsing. There is something in the physical form and weight of a published book that validates its reality, gives it substance. Allowing yourself a small, congratulatory smile, you idly note a good-looking trio of cosplayers pass right by the front of the table, acutely aware that you're consciously delaying the inevitable; your procrastination irks you.

You doggedly target the cosplayers, refusing the memory center stage. They look vaguely like fresh TV matinee idols or perhaps Bench fashion models, skin unblemished, muscles all toned and sculpted. The couple, holding hands as they pass, are dressed as Bathala and Adarna, while their companion, trailing behind them, has come as Zsa-Zsa Zaturnnah. All look the part they've chosen, and appropriately enough, you're not entirely certain what the sex of the Zsa-Zsa cosplayer is, and that puts you in mind of many things, things like mystery and ambiguity; things that demand shrilly for attention, like a hungry cat yowling...

The call.

You received it on your mobile earlier this morning, just as you sat down at the table, thirty minutes before the gates were scheduled to open.

It was the *karibang*, calling from a landline, if the reception was any indication. He spoke about your book, and you wish you could use some of the things he said as back-cover blurbs.

"It reminds me of the old days," the little man said, a strange, alien tone to his words. (You would, later on, identify the tone as one of *glee*.) "I've told all my friends about it, and they're busy getting their own copies too. Particularly those who are actually *in* it. I told all of them: 'If you have a problem with how you're portrayed, take it up with me. *I* told the stories. Any apparent inconsistencies or fallacies are entirely my fault.'

"It's made waves, your book. It's caught the attention of so very many. As I'm sure you meant it to."

You remained silent. You'd known the moment had arrived;

the moment when you'd be unmasked.

"It was always about those final stories, wasn't it?" the *karibang* went on. "*Those* were the stories you were waiting to hear. That's why you decided to stop after that last one. By then, you'd gotten what you'd wanted."

And then, listening to that voice that resonated with the sound of rubble and darkness, you recalled (as you do now), that sense of *revelation*, that sense of the past, of *tales* from the past, finally flowering open before you, disclosing the truths that had always been there.

The little man's stories . . . They were your *lola*'s stories, strange tales of wondrous and terrible beauty. Stories she claimed were about your family, about your ancestors, about *her* ancestors. Stories that were, at times, *ambiguous*; some seemingly about people *other* than the ones she was actually talking about.

The *karibang* hadn't said it, but it was clear: *he knew*.

You wanted to make him understand that none of it had been conscious; you honestly hadn't been aware of these motives until after the book had been assembled and published, reading it for the first time in its final form of dead trees and glue. That was when you realized what it had all really been for; the talking, the listening, the story after story after story, waiting to hear the ones that would unlock generations-old secrets.

You wanted to say all of this, and more, despite the fact that somehow, you felt that he already knew this, that he knew that there was no premeditation, on *your* part, at least.

But in your silence, the little man continued to speak: "Understand that this is the way of stories. They're always about something, even if what they're about isn't the story itself.

"All you humans have both light *and* dark within you. You have the capacity to commit acts motivated by one or the other.

What you are about to receive is an understanding of where you came from, not who you're meant to be.

"Just think of the Skin. Of where it came from, and what part of it was eventually used for."

There was silence then, and you imagined you could hear the sound of ages passing, of time and the pointed scattering of its detritus.

"The book is excellent. Congratulations."

The little man hung up then, and you knew why he'd called you today, of all days, even if the book had been out for over a month now.

A year and a day.

Like he'd said, the book had caught the attention of so very many. Including, you imagine, the one whose attention it had been meant to catch in the first place.

Somewhere out there, a copy of *Alamatia* is being considered, and weighed, the name gracing its spine burning itself into someone's eyes (and how many eyes exactly, you're not really sure at the moment).

Tonight. Tonight, you'll know for certain. A knot in your stomach twists, tightens.

But you close your own eyes, and breathe in, then out, slowly, allowing the familiar noises of a con to cradle you, to remind you of who you are.

You will look upon *eyes* tonight; the electric blue of a single pair, or the noisome green of seven. Whichever you will see tonight, whatever happens to open its arms to you, it will be whatever it will be. Whatever it already *is*. Whatever it has been for centuries.

The only question now is, Will you embrace it back?

You smile, open your eyes, flip the fresh copy of *Alamatia* open to its flyleaf, and heft your pen, prepared to accept the price for illumination.

SALAKEP

A Door Opens:
The Beginning of the Fall of
the Ispancialo-in-Hinirang

Dean Francis Alfar

Dean Francis Alfar is a leading advocate of speculative fiction in the Philippines, and the publisher of the annual "Philippine Speculative Fiction" anthology. His novel "Salamanca" won both the Book Development Association of the Philippines' Gintong Aklat award, as well as the Grand Prize in the Don Carlos Palanca Memorial Awards for Literature. He has nine more Palancas to his name, two Manila Critics' Circle National Book Awards, the Philippine Free Press Literary Award, and the Philippine Graphic/Fiction Award. His short fiction has been collected in "The Kite of the Stars and Other Stories", and "How to Traverse Terra Incognita", and been published in venues both national and international, including "The Year's Best Fantasy & Horror", "Rabid Transit: Menagerie", "Latitude", and "The Apex Book of World SF."

It seemed fitting to end the anthology with this story. Sometimes, I feel like there's a tendency—even amongst Filipinos—to view the Philippines as a footnote on the world stage. Yet there's so much that is unique and beautiful in Philippine culture, if only we would take the time to learn it. Philippine mythology has much to offer the world. This anthology, we hope, has opened a doorway. We invite you to step through it.

Over a century before the Final Revolution that ended the Ispancialo rule in Hinirang[1], there was an obscure uprising that almost brought the colonizers to their knees[2]. Archival discoveries in the past 50 years[3] have brought to light the sequences of events that have been characterized as "The Door Uprising"[4]. Inveterate diarists and letter-writers, the Ispancialo who were aware of the uprising provided copious details—enough to inspire a goodly number of popular novels[5] and films[6].

In 1784, a Door in the Katao faithlands was opened by chance by a student[7]. The audienca royal of Hinirang, includ-

---

[1] The Ispancialo ruled for 327 years.

[2] There were frequent uprisings by the Katao of Hinirang, who resented the Ispancialo's *encomienda* system. Among the most dangerous ones occurred in 1589, when the first Ispancialo governor, Miguel López de Legazpi, was made a viceroy, with the subsequent appointment of the *audienca royal*. At the height of the religious mass to commemorate the event, over 80 Katao, armed only with stones, attacked the assemblage, ultimately falling to superior Ispancialo numbers and weaponnry.

Norhata Kudarat, *Colonial Hinirang*, 1565-1653 (Mirabilis Press, 1991), 107.

[3] Alberto Manalastas, "Historal Trove Unearthed in Diliman," *Diario* Manila [Ciudad Manila, Hinirang], December 11, 2003.

[4] Certain revisionist scholars such as Meynard Bolasco and Gabriel Lo-tonon prefer the use of the term "gate".

[5] The first such novel was "Sangria Yesterday" by Nolledo Patalinjug, winner of the Carlos Palanca Memorial Award Grand Prize for Novel in 1981, and published by Anvil Books in 1982.

[6] Among the most notable is "The Blood Door", the critically-acclaimed 2002 Hinirang-Nippon film directed by Satoshi Kon.

[7] It was Alonzo Nicolas Clessidraña of the Concilio Ciencia who discovered the door to the Katao's faithlands.

Alonzo, researching the chronal peculiarities of the forbidden area underneath the Plaza Emperyal, stumbled across the forgotten wooden opening

ing representatives from the military, religious, arcane, poetic[8]
and scientific[9], decided to shut the door[10] by sending an expe-

---

on his thirty-third day of investigation, just before he was about to aban-
don his pursuit of a degree at the Orden and instead help his grandfather
maintain his shop along the Encantó lu Caminata.

Instead, despite the fervent protests of his research companions, he forced
open the odd looking door, using the *calipher resonancia*, and vanished into
the unearthly radiance. Those who were left behind, after a painful and
hurried discussion, shut and barred the wooden aperture, and rushed to
report everything to their superiors.

Victor Montes, Gregorio Lacuesta, Wilfredo Co, *Uprisings* (Best Day
Publishing, 1989), 23.

[8] Masters of the Spoken Word, the Poetics were versed in many secret meth-
ods of power, such as what would in later decades be characterized as the
bildungsroman form of twisting moral identities and the use of inveterate
haplology and edulcoration.

[9] Realizing that the situation was beyond their capacity to handle, the Concilio Ciencia sent emissaries to the other members of the *audienca royal*
of Ciudad Meiora—the Secular, Poetic, Arcane and Spiritual institutions
whose policies and movements decided the fate of Ispancialo Hinirang—
requesting an emergency meeting to determine what needed to be done.
The missive stated in no uncertain terms that secrecy was required due to
the delicate nature of the situation and that it was imperative that all five
Powers convened immediately.

Carol Tan and Marlene Trinidad, eds., Power Plays: The Balance of
Power in Colonial Hinirang (Ateneo Press), 1983.

[10] First to arrive at the squat red towers of the Concilio Ciencia was an unre-
markable qalesa bearing two extraordinary men. Alejandro Baltran Alessio
du Verrada ei Ramirez, the Guvernador-Henerale of Hinirang, eschewed
his normal accoutrements of rank and wore a dull-colored cloak over simple vestments. He was accompanied by Ser Humberto Carlos Pietrado ei
Villareal, the elder brother of the man who had recently, rather embarrassingly, lost a peculiar footrace against a Katao woman. They represented the
Military Government, the most visible of the Powers.

A few minutes later, a velvet-covered palanquin brought the representatives of the Gremio Poetica. Betina du Zabala, the Most Excellent Primo
Orador, gestured impatiently at her companion to hurry out of the con-
veyance. Biting back her tongue, Esperanza du Zabala, the Most Excellent

Segundo Orador, locked vicious gazes with her mother, and rushed into the Orden's tower. Both Oradors, recently arrived from the Mother Country, were masters of Poetics, and the Gremio Poetica held sway over all art and communication in the Ispancialo demesne.

Maestra Onsia Helmina and Maestro Cinco Almario, of the Escolia du Arcana Menor, arrived next, on foot. Maestra Helmina clutched her robes close to her breast and looked up to try to read the thoughts of her reluctant younger companion. But Maestro Almario, rumored to have Katao blood in his veins, kept his silence. So, without a word, the representatives of the Arcane surreptitiously erected invisible wards around themselves and entered the tower.

The last to arrive were a pair from the Katedral Grandu, divinely-inspired clerics of the *Tres Hermanas* and spiritual heirs of the Pio Familia. Madre Gorospe invoked her eighty-six years of Faith to calm herself down, inwardly trembling at the implications hinted at by the summoning missive. But her companion, the Tiq'barang cleric Sister Veronica T'gubilin, smiled in anticipation and stomped her hooves once to contain her excitement.

Within the red towers, Consejal Lucio Pejeno, current head of the Concilio Ciencia, ushered all the leaders in after requesting for them to leave their companions in an outer room.

"Thank you all for responding so quickly," Consejal Lucio Pejeno began. "Forgive the terse nature of the letter I sent. The sensitive nature of –"

"Yes, yes," interrupted Maestra Onsia Helmina of the Escolia Arcana. "Obviously you have stumbled across something important enough to summon all five of us from our duties. Tell us."

"You must forgive the Maestra for her characteristic mordacious tone, Consejal Pejeno," Betina du Zabala of the Gremio Poetica said, smiling oddly. "She would be more eloquent, but is, no doubt, as curious as the rest of us as to the nature of your call."

"Of course, Excellencies, of course," Consejal Pejeno stared at his hands briefly and stated simply, "We have found a portal to Hinirang's heaven."

"What?" Madre Gorospe suddenly felt the weight of her years upon her body, and stifled a yearning to scream in horror. She closed her eyes but saw only blood and tears.

"It is of great interest to the mother Church, naturally," Consejal Pejeno began.

"It is of great interest to us all, Consejal." The Guvernador-Henerale rose from his seat and gently touched the arm of Madre Gorospe, who, eyes shut tight, was shaking noticeably. She opened her teary eyes and nodded her thanks. "Where is this portal?"

"Beneath the Plaza Empyral, Your Excellency," Consejal Pejeno replied.

"Imagine that," Betina du Zabala spoke to no one in particular. "Is it open?" she asked Consejal Pejeno.

"Yes."

"Who opened it?" asked Maestra Helmina. "Or was it open already?"

"One of my own, a young student, opened the door," the Consejal admitted.

"And?" Betina du Zabala asked softly.

"And he vanished," the Consejal replied.

"What makes you so certain that it is a gateway to the Hinirang faithlands?" Madre Gorospe asked.

"Our instruments recorded the presence of the Ether," the Consejal sat back wearily. "As you all know, that signifies the presence of faithlands, as proven by our apparatus at the conquest of Nueva Mundo when we—" ,

"No one here doubts the veracity of your report nor the integrity of the instruments guided by your scientific principles, dear Ser," the Guvernador-Henerale said. "So there is a door. An open door. You were correct to call us all. We must decide our cause of action immediately."

"Then we vote," Betina du Zabala said firmly.

"Yes. Yes, we do," agreed Madre Gorospe, shaking her head sadly, for she knew what position she had to take.

"Very well. As is our custom, I will ask each of you to formally state your decision," Consejal Pejeno said. "I will begin."

"I, Lucio Pejeno, Consejal Temporal, speak for the Concilio Ciencia," the heavy-set man said. "I say shut the door. Science has no interest in the indio faithland. We were the ones who discovered and opened the door. We will shut it as well."

He gestured to the others. "Who speaks for the Poetics?"

"I, Betina du Zabala, Most Excellent Primo Orador, speak for the Gremio Poetica," the fiercely beautiful woman spoke, her mellifluous voice perfectly pitched and resonant. "I say enter the door. We can navigate what is beyond and find the source of their tales—mostly primitive and pathetic folkloric drivel, from what little we have heard since my office arrived in these humid islands last year. And we take it in the name of Ispancia. Thereafter, only our narratives will exist in this misbegotten land."

"Who speaks for the Arcane?"

"I, Onsia Helmina, Maestra Honoria, speak for both schools," the silver-haired woman said, considering her next words carefully. "I say enter ditionary force through the portal. What occurred next was a massacre[11], as the expeditionary force found itself assaulted by the heroes of the Katao's folk belief system[12]. Though a few

---

the door. But only to study, always only to study. We must preserve what the indios have, and learn to share in their culture. What we learn we can use to improve upon what we already know."

"Who speaks for the Spiritual?"

"I, Madre Gorospe, Faithful of the Tres Hermanas, speak for the Mother Church in Hinirang," the old cleric responded, her words heavy with sorrow. "I say enter the door. Destroy the pagan faithlands."

"Who speaks for the Secular?"

"I, Alejandro Ramirez, Guvernador-Henerale of Hinirang, speak for the Government," the dark-haired man spoke quietly. "I say shut the door. But if it means entering it to close it, then I recommend that as well. We will protect the interests of our citizenry. Having an open doorway in the midst of our Ciudad is unacceptable. It must be shut."

Lakangiting Lopez, Selma Dornilla, Ponciano Abadilla, *Reconstructing History Vol. 5: The Unpublished Letters of Amado Pejeno* (Hinirang University Press, 1995), 78-84.

[11] Alonto grossly exaggerates and misuses the term "massacre". Though over a hundred people are believed to have perished, this is nothing compared to the infamous Tsino Massacre of 1603 (also known as the Sangley Uprising or Three Mandarins Massacre), where, fearing the growing Tsino population, the Ispancialo soldiers under the command of Governor-General Pedro Bravo de Acuña slew over 20,000.

[12] The hundred-man expeditionary force, led by the juniors of the audienca royal, entered the Door and found themselves covered from head to toe in thick Ether.

"Keep your formation," Ser Humberto Carlos Pietrado ei Villareal shouted in the dimness.

An eerie silence permeated the surroundings after the men shouted their assent.

"Be wary," Sister Veronica T'gubilin of the Katedral Grandu whispered to Maestro Cinco Almario of the Escolia du Arcana Menor.

"Believe me, I have my wards at ready, Sister," the young man replied with a shiver in his voice.

"Pejeno!" Ser Humberto spoke sharply. "Is there anything your ciencia can tell us? My men need something to attack!"

"Patience, please, Ser," Jovito Pejeno mumbled, his sweaty hands tinkering with instrumentation he could barely see, inwardly cursing the head of the Concilio Ciencia, his very uncle, who assigned him to accompany the expeditionary force. "These delicate things take some time and I cannot—"

"Do you see that? That light," Esperanza du Zabala, the Most Excellent Segundo Orador, said softly, pointing at a reddish glow in the distance.

"It is a man," Sister Veronica said, squinting her eyes. "We should—"

A shout like thunder resounded through the Ether, and the Heroes of Hinirang were revealed.

The voice belonged to Banna of the Calingga, handsome and radiant on a floating cloud that flashed crimson. In his right arm he brandished Diwaton, the axe that followed his every command.

On Banna's right stood the demi-god Labaw Donggon of the Bisayas, holding high the crystal sphere that enabled him supernatural sight.

On Banna's left was the mighty Lam-ang of the Iluko, his chest covered with powerful amulets, holding a great spear. Around him swirled powerful winds, ready to obey his words, disrupting the Ether.

There stood Prince Bantugan of the unconquered Maranao, accompanied by his spirit daimon Magaw, his powerful hands restraining a fearsome crocodile whose loyalty he'd won.

More heroes were revealed as the Ether dissipated.

There, the resplendent Suban-on hero, Sandayo, his fingers shiny with rings—each of which contained a person he's previously pressed into it.

There, Kundaman of Palaoan, his slender build belying his potent magic.

There, Tanagyaw of the Agyu, raising his golden cane.

There, Tulalang, the Dragon Slayer, with his black shield.

There, Tuwaang of the Manuvu, lightning crackling at his fingertips, the center of his forehead as bright as a star.

The Ispancialo expeditionary force stood stunned.

"Take them, my brothers!" Banna shouted, releasing Diwaton from his grip.

It was the last thing Jovito Pejeno saw, as it split him in half before attacking the soldiers.

"Attack!" Ser Humberto Carlos Pietrado ei Villareal commanded his men, shaking them out their stupor.

As the heroes closed in, chaos ensued, Ispancialo steel meeting Katao metal.

Maestro Cinco Almario of the Escolia du Arcana Menor watched in shock as Labaw Donggon moved toward him. He fought to recall his most powerful wards, running the arcane syllables over and over in his mind before he spoke them, fearful of the untoward results an untimely catachresis could produce. A glimmering blue sphere enveloped him and he sighed in relief when Labaw Donggon stopped at its periphery.

"You cannot harm me! Leave! Leave!" Maestro Cinco half shouted, half pleaded. "This is the finest arcana!"

Labaw Donggon just shook his head and smiled, raising the brilliant to his eyes. "I see it broken, this little shield of yours."

Maestro Cinco's death cry resounded as his arcane sphere collapsed around him, shredding his body into many pieces.

When the heroes ran towards the expeditionary force, Sister Veronica began to pray, filling her spirit with the power of her faith, imploring the Tres Hermanas to grant her the power to swat aside the pagans. But the Tres Hermanas were deaf to her pleas, though her life was somewhat spared. She screamed from her confines in one of Sandayo's many rings.

"You're mine now," Sandayo calmly informed her as he dispatched a soldier.

It was Esperanza du Zabala, the Most Excellent Segundo Orador, who kept her wits about her, launching into a staccato recitation that created a field of powerful words around her immediate area. As the invisible words engulfed them, Tulalang, Tanagyaw and Tuwaang fought against a sudden hebetude that threatened to swallow them in the throes of dull ennui.

Struggling to maintain her control, Esperanza tried to see where Ser Humberto was, to tell him that this was madness, that they, yes, even she, were ill-prepared, and that a retreat was a better option, if not the only option.

But Ser Humberto was busy fighting for his life. With a group of men that grew smaller and smaller with every moment, he faced Kundaman and Prince Bantugan.

"Stand your ground, men!" he shouted, forcing his way to Prince Bantugan. But before he could close in the handsome man, Prince Bantugan gestured sharply to his side. The giant crocodile snapped its jaws and devoured Ser Humberto whole.

Seeing this, Esperanza began to run back toward the Door, still articulating words to keep the heroes around her weakened.

"I'm sorry, brothers, but I grow sleepy," Tulalang said to Tanagyaw and Tuwaang with a yawn. Tanagyaw growled and Tuwaang shouted as they fought the wearisome effects.

"But not to worry," Tulalang mumbled as he closed his eyes. "My shield will fight for me . . ."

survivors managed to escape and shut the Door, the damage was already done.

For the next hundred years, native storytellers all over the archipelago began telling the old heroic tales[13], blurring geographical and tribal lines with heroes from the north appearing in southern tales, and vice versa[14]. This undermined the Ispancialo strategy of "divide and conquer" by which clannish tribes were set against each other, effectively quelling disturbances[15]. However, the heroic tales, in which heroes from different tribes and traditions joined forces, continued to spread, leading to a gradual and inevitable sense of nationalism[16].

This culminated in the famous 1896 Revolution[17] when at last the Katao overthrew Ispancialo rule, followed by the

---

Tulalang's black shield flew from his arm and chased after the fleeing Esperanza. When the door was almost within her reach, Esperanza turned around to take one last look at the terrible attack the expeditionary force had suffered. And fell backward into the open Door, knocked senseless when Tulalang's black shield slammed into her.

(Esperanza du Zabala's account of the event ends here. She, and four soldiers who had managed to escape in the early parts of the assault, were the only survivors.)

Langgit Sikat, *Palatandaan: The Memoirs of Esperanza du Zabala*, trans. Amir al-Raban Lane (MSU, 1975), 146-150

[13] See the *Hinirang Folk Literature Series*, compiled and edited by Damian Eusebio (Hinirang University Press, 1982) for examples. Of particular interest are the materials found in Vol. VIII, *The Epics*.

[14] Rowan Go, ed., *Word of Mouth: The Transmission of Heroic Tales* (Boston: Houghton Mifflin), 1998.

[15] Leonardo Villavicencio, *Ispaniola: Strategies of Governance* (New York: Cambridge University Press, 2000), 42.

[16] Bienvenido Rafanan, "Troubled Waters: The Influence of the Tale," in Crispin Reyes, ed., *Hinirang: A Colonial History* (Georgetown: Blackwell, 2003), 265-271.

[17] José Protasio Rizal Mercado ei Alonso Realonda, founder of *La Liga Hinirang* and a rallying figure for government reform was executed, which triggered the Hinirang Revolution spearheaded by Andres Bonifacio y de

declaration of an independent and sovereign Hinirang in 1898[18].

Castro and Emilio Aguinaldo ei Famy, founders of "KATAO", better known as "The Brotherhood".

[18] The short-lived Republic was interrupted by the Ispancialo-Americano War.

Remembrance

Eliza Victoria

Eliza Victoria was gracious enough to provide us with an additional story for this expanded print edition of Alternative Alamat. It's set in the same universe as "Ana's Little Pawnshop on Makiling St.", although only one character really overlaps.

This story features Hukloban. While I mentioned in Appendix A that she is technically a mortal agent of Sitan, not a goddess, it's not uncommon to see her portrayed as such (I doubt anyone who met her was in a position to quibble much over technicalities) and Eliza portrays her as such here.

It was raining. The city buses were as congested as the roads, and Stella squeezed into the bus to stand in the aisle with the other passengers too unlucky to get a seat. Wet umbrellas and soaked jackets pressed against her cheek and shins. Ensconced in a sea of people, she thought, If a bomb explodes or if someone starts shooting, I'll have nowhere to hide.

What a strange thought to have.

There was someone holding her hand. She looked down and saw herself. Herself, Stella, Happy Stella, holding her hand. She looked into Happy Stella's eyes and felt, not the sensation of joy, but the quiet hum of comfort. A constant, steady thrum, like the knowledge of the sun in the sky, of the timeless location of home.

She held Happy Stella's hand, and realized: This is Kaitlin's memory. So that was how Kaitlin felt about her. This is so unfair, Stella thought.

All of a sudden, Hukluban was standing beside her. "Beautiful, isn't it?"

Startled, Stella pulled herself away. The glass marble of Kaitlin's memory sat on her open palm. On her lap was the velvet drawstring pouch. Inside were more glass marbles. Hundreds more. Hukluban, beguiling as always in her short black dress, sat in front of Stella.

"Do you have everything you need?" she said. Everything about Hukluban reminded Stella of fire. Her red eyes shone like burning comets. Her scent was that of burning coals. Stella felt like choking.

They were on the rooftop of an abandoned twenty-storey hotel in Manila. Stella didn't know what the hotel had been called, but Hukluban had said it was the perfect spot.

"Yes," Stella said, her eyes bloodshot, her joints aching from lack of sleep.

"Very well." Hukluban stood up and smoothed down her dress. Her red heels clacked on the cement as she approached the edge of the roof. She glanced over a shoulder, smiled. "I shall see you soon."

Hukluban jumped and turned into a flock of black doves. The doves flew away over the slumbering city, into the night. Piteousness, Stella thought. A piteousness of doves. That's what they are called. Kaitlin taught me that.

A murder of crows.

A murder.

Pity me.

Stella cried.

When her sobs subsided, she took another glass marble. Stella let her consciousness enter its sphere the way Hukluban taught her, placing it on her open palm and concentrating—

Stella was herself, as a fresh graduate and a new employee. She was sitting in a dining room, facing a trio of angry women. Her father had punched another man during a drunken brawl And the women, relatives of the injured man, were demanding ten thousand pesos. Ten thousand pesos, and they wouldn't press charges. Her father, recently unemployed, had been involved in one fight after another in the town. Prior to this incident, Stella's family had managed to hush up the injured parties with baked goods and a civilized dinner, but not this time. Ten thousand pesos or jail. It was a big amount for Stella, who still lived as a bedspacer on campus. That was roughly equivalent to six months of rent. Or several new dresses, ten hardbound books, DVD boxed sets, things she wouldn't buy for herself because she had to "save for the future". This is what family means, she thought, as her heart filled with hatred. You live your life with honor and kindness, and someone else will make you pay for their mistakes as they tarnish your name.

She said as much to her mother, who then damned Stella for her pride. "You listen to me –"

But that's where the memory stopped. There was a crack in the marble. It appeared that Stella had already erased her mother's words from her memory, a long time ago.

Stella tried another marble.

Summer. Sampaguita blossoms inching through the bamboo slats of her aunt's fence. She saw herself, little Stella, aged six, running down the unpaved driveway in mud-spattered clothes. "Tatay!" the child shouted, jumping into Stella's arms. Her father's arms. It was her father's memory. Stella felt as though she were mourning a friend that had yet to die. Take care of this, Stella thought, caressing the child's back. This won't last. And it didn't, it didn't. Stella pulled away from the marble.

Another marble. It was late afternoon, and Stella was sitting on the sofa watching a soap opera. Stella watched as the crying women onscreen were pre-empted by a breaking news bulletin. Whose memory was this? Her mother's? One of her aunts? Stella watched as the reporter gave early details about a developing story. One shot dead in botched bus heist. Stella didn't feel anything. It was one news story among many. She waited for the soap opera to resume.

The next marble was clearly her mother's. She watched another young Stella, aged nine, crying over a school project—a homemade comic book—that she had to finish by that same afternoon. Stella helped the little girl spread pastel on the crude drawings. Stella wanted to soothe her. She wanted to tell the little girl that some sorrows were temporary, that some of life's pains seemed insurmountable but often meant nothing.

Another marble. Hers. Kaitlin was holding her hand. Stella watched as a large group of people got off the bus. The aisle cleared, and a couple of seats—three rows from the exit—became available, and they both stood up and claimed them. Stella sat near the window. "Let's go to the mall today," Kaitlin whispered in her ear. "Let's grab some dinner." A man sitting behind the driver stood up, but instead of climbing down, he faced the passengers. For a split-second Stella wondered what he was doing. "Sure," Stella told Kaitlin, and Kaitlin smiled. The man took out a gun.

Stella and Kaitlin held onto each other as the man walked down the aisle, demanding the passengers' wallets and cell phones as he waved the gun in their faces. "Give me the bag," the man said. Kaitlin at the time had her camera, an ebook reader, and a new smartphone. Even here, in this cruel rerun, Stella still couldn't tell what caused it. Did Kaitlin hesitate? Was the man a neophyte criminal, easily provoked? Stella heard the now-familiar explosion in her ear as the gun dislodged a single bullet into Kaitlin's right eye. Stella pulled away before the screaming began.

Friend. That was how the news articles referred to her. Not girlfriend. Never girlfriend. At the funeral she approached Kaitlin's sisters and said I loved her, and they patted her hand and said Of course, of course. We loved her, too.

Stella saw that there was a glass marble in the pouch that looked different from the rest. Stella found herself sitting on a warm bench, the wind blowing through her hair. Where am I? she thought. I don't remember this.

Something was coming. She could feel it. Something grand. Something that would change her life and make her happy again. Oh, she thought to herself, smiling, waiting. Here it is. Here it comes.

"You're not supposed to remember that one."

Stella pulled away from the memory in surprise. A woman with radiant curls, wearing jeans and a white shirt, was sitting behind her. She had her chin in her hand, elbow on her knee. Her eyes contained swirling galaxies instead of pupils.

"That's a future memory."

"I'm going to jump off this building," Stella told her. She raised the pouch, the glass marbles clinking inside. "I'm going to bring these with me."

"All your memories," the woman said, "and every memory of you. An elegant way of erasing the fact that you ever existed. Hukluban's handiwork, I presume?"

Tala pointed at the glass marbles. Stella couldn't respond.

"What is your name?"

"Stella."

"What a beautiful name!" she said. "No wonder I was drawn to you. My name is Tala." Tala looked back at the marbles. "Only the shapeshifter, the goddess of death, has the power to turn memory into something else. I have seen memories turned into wood and rock. But glass? Very elegant. Very poetic. And for her to let a future one slip into the bag… very cunning. Was it to taunt you with what you'd miss? To make you question whether it could ever happen? Or, instead, perhaps—?"

Stella cried.

"Why do you grieve," Tala said, "when you've just held hope in your hands?"

"I can't stand this any longer," Stella said.

"But you can. In one sense, you already have. It may be in ten years, or next Tuesday, but if you're still here, then somewhere, sometime, you'll make that memory." Tala took the pouch and held the marble to her eye. "You mortals are strange, with your sadness. Your grief is just a blip in the universe, but it is, at the same time, enormous."

"I'll get better?" Stella said.

Tala stood up.

She lifted the drawstring pouch, and the glass marbles rose to the sky, arching like the glowing band of the Milky Way, all save one, which Tala kept.

Stella blinked, and wondered how she'd gotten … wherever she was. She looked up, and stared. Somehow, the stars looked brighter than ever.

Years later, a woman lay on the sands of a beach.

The wind blew through her hair. Oh, she thought. She sat up straight. She felt a thrill, a familiar bliss. Here it is, she thought. She closed her book. She smiled, ready. Here it comes.

Appendix A:
A Few Notable Philippine Deities

The Philippines doesn't have one pantheon of gods, but several. What we've attempted to do here is give you a glimpse of some of the more unique deities, either because of the stories told about them, or their areas of dominion. These are the gods and goddesses interpreted visually by Mervin Malonzo in this anthology, and I list them here in that same order. I've also noted the region/community that worshipped the deity (or the version of the deity that I describe), as well as a short description.

Balitok—Ifugao—Son of Bugan of the Skyworld and Kinggauan, a mortal man. Due to the separation of his parents, he was eventually split in half: the upper half became a celestial being, and the lower half was converted into the animals that populate the Earth.

Bangunbangun—Sulod/Panay—God of Universal Time, the deity who regulated the movements of the cosmos.

Dadanhayan ha Sugay—Bukidnon—His name means "The Lord from Whom Permission is Asked." He is also called Takinan Manawbanaw ("Chief who Owns the Drooling Saliva") and Gumagang-aw ("Ten-headed"). He was one of the three beings who resided in the circle of absolute brightness, the Bulbulusan Balugtu, which existed before earth or heaven.

He created the six Incantus who watch over the cosmos, and was instrumental in the creation of heaven and earth.

Dagau—Manobo—a goddess who set the world atop five iron pillars. Dagau lived amongst these pillars with her monstrous pet python, and she had the ability to cause earthquakes by ordering the python to writhe around the pillars. She was said to hate war, and would cause earthquakes when the blood from those slain in war would leak through the soil and drip on her face.

Haliya—Bicol—Haliya is the Bicolano goddess of the moon and protector of women. She is sometimes described as wearing a mask, and battling Bakonawa, the evil serpent who seeks to swallow the moon.

The Halupe—Ifugao—A class of deities known as the "Spirits of Remembrance". These deities remind people of obligations, such as debts, and are believed to be benevolent, even if they do specialize in the ability to control memory and emotion.

Hukloban—Tagalog—Not a goddess per se, but one of the four mortal agents of Sitan (the god who ruled Kasanaan, where souls were tortured), and the one rumored to be the most powerful. She was capable of taking any form, and could kill—or heal—a person with a wave of her hand, or destroy a house by using words alone.

Malaon/Makapatag—Visayas—This is a supreme deity with (at least) two aspects: as Malaon, the Ancient One, the deity was female, mild, and understanding; as Makapatag, the Leveler, the deity was male, austere, and feared. It's possible that this duality stems from foreigners equating the supreme female

God of one community with the supreme male God of another.

Melu—Bilaan—Melu was a being so large that he could not be compared with any known thing. He had gold teeth and was obsessed with cleanliness, so much so that he turned white from his constant scrubbing of his skin. Eventually, the dead skin which sloughed from his body when he scrubbed it accumulated to such a degree that he decided he must make some use of the skin . . . so he used it to make the Earth.

Patag'aes—Sulod—Patag'aes is one of three deities who determine the time and manner of death of all mortals. Each of the three has a very specific task: one ascertains birth, the next observes if the child was born alive. Lastly, Patag'aes converses with the newborn baby to find out how long it wants to live, and how it wishes to die. This is a conversation that no one should overhear, because should Patag'aes realize that someone is eavesdropping, he will kill the infant himself.

The Salakep—Tagbanwa—The Salakep are the deities of epidemic and sickness, who dwell in the Kiyabusan, the void beyond the sky-world. When the northeast wind blows into the islands, they sail through the air in their ships, and spread disease, taking the dead with them back to Kiyabusan. Those who die during epidemics are said to have been consumed by the Salakep. The Salakep are described as small, dark and kinky-haired, their faces and bodies covered with small round scars.

Appendix B:
Interview with Professor
Herminia Meñez Coben

Professor Herminia Meñez Coben has a Ph.D. in Folklore and Folklife from the University of Pennsylvania, was Professor of American Multicultural Studies at California State University, Sonoma, and taught "Philippine Folklore and Society" at the University of California, Los Angeles. She is the author of "Folklore Communication Among Filipinos in California" (1980), "Explorations in Philippine Folklore" (1996) and "Verbal Arts in Philippine Indigenous Communities: Poetics, Society, and History" (2009).

You were exposed to many Philippine myths and folktales through stories told by your parents and nursemaids during the period during World War II when you were hiding out in the mountains. Do you think that encountering those stories under such intense circumstances could account for your fascination with them?

I was only five years old at the outbreak of the second World War. My remembrances of those years spent in Agcawilan, where we had evacuated, are full of wonder and a sense of adventure. It was a whole new world for me and my brother as we explored the forested mountain above our house, and the rice fields below, where we played and swam! Our nursemaids who evacuated with us told us stories about beautiful women—*Ingkanto*, or "fairies"—who dwelt in the *Nunok*—or Ficus trees—and in the riverstreams. Those images [of fairies], of course, were pre-Disney, as we had not even been to the movies yet, and so we could let our imagination run wild and create magical beings and creatures of midnight who would later haunt our dreams. The war, however, was not a source of anxiety for us children, although I imagine our parents were deeply anxious and afraid each time the Japanese bombed our town in the distance.

Do you have any favorites from the stories you've encountered in your studies of the various indigenous oral traditions?
My favorite stories and characters come from the epics. [The epics featured] women warriors, certainly, but also characters such as Mungan, the shaman from the Bukidnon and Ilianen Manobo. Leper and healer both, she gives her people the betelnut of immortality, which enables them to ascend to the Skyworld, while she remains on earth forever to guide future inhabitants on the path toward a life without death. I think that one of the short stories I'll write will be about her.

The performance of verbal art has traditionally occurred in a social context. In "Verbal Art", you mention that this is why such performance both reflects and transforms social life. What role do you see (or would you want to see) oral storytelling playing in the lives of people of today, particularly young people?
Today, television—not storytelling—has become the center of the lives of children, as far as entertainment goes. Certainly, media have the power to transform our lives, and influence our views of the world. Even the games of childhood have been replaced by video games. Those are certainly different

ways of socialization.

What about the role/importance of stories of the fantastic? You've mentioned before that "[f]olklore empowers its users to create an alternative persona."

Fantasy is very important for personal growth. Myths, legends, and folktales provide fantastic stimuli for the imagination, and allow people to create an alternative persona. When I was a child, I imagined myself as the heroine of the *koridos* ... I even changed my name to "Maria", the epitome of beauty and goodness. To make sure my playmates recognized my new identity, I wore a star on my forehead, to distinguish myself from her evil sisters, Isabel and Catalina. [But] these *koridos* were long, involved narratives set in Europe, so that one had to imagine the characters to be European! This is a topic I dealt with in an essay in "Explorations in Philippine Folklore".

In both your books you've cast a spotlight on warrior heroines from our oral epics, which I appreciate because people don't seem to be as aware of them as their male counterparts. Why do you think heroines such as Matabagka, Bolak Sonday, and Emla have faded from public awareness?

Let's be frank: Was there any real interest in our epics and epic heroines to begin with? Our own literary writers, at least in the past, were not interested in verbal art as literature, as a veritable mother lode of imagery and metaphor that could enrich Philippine fiction and poetry. I hope that "Verbal Arts" can in some small fashion help point the way.

Aside from the warrior heroines, do you have any other favorite characters from our oral traditions? In your chapter on the Bukidnon in "Verbal Arts", you explored in some depth the characters of Sawalan (a warrior but one at odds with the

heroes) and Mungan (a shaman).

My favorite characters from the indigenous oral epics have to be the warrior heroines from the Guman and the Bukidnon. But I also like Agyu because he is primarily a warrior, he is a great leader who takes his people to paradise. He also is an artist, weaving his own knee bands, etc., and he allows his sister to fight with him in the battlefield, much like the heroine of the hudhud. Mungan, the shaman, is richly portrayed in the Bukidnon Ulahingan, as leper and healer, musician and leader.

One of the elements that made "Verbal Arts" so unique for me was the fact that you took the time to point out aspects of each culture that were similar to others—and in the instances where there was a divergence, you tried to explain why that was the case. Other books might classify the societies that engaged in headhunting, but not many would emphasize that the practice served a different purpose for the Ifugao (to receive prestige and a bountiful harvest) than it did for the Isneg and Kalinga (to receive health and protection). Do you think that in trying to emphasize commonalities, or generalize a "Pre-Hispanic Philippines" (as some books have done in the past) there is a danger of homogenizing what are in fact, very diverse cultures and peoples?

My concern in presenting the verbal arts traditions individually was to underscore the differences, so that one could appreciate the complexities of practices such as headhunting, for instance, but at the same time see similarities that represent cultural patterns which unify various ethnicities. Also, a very important point: in presenting the poetry, rather than simply providing ethnographic descriptions, I wanted to show how verbal artists, in their own words, expressed their views of themselves and their art.

Given the number of different cultures that call our archipelago home, it seems inevitable that there will be popular misconceptions about these cultures and traditions. Have you encountered any of these in your research, and if so what are the most pernicious?

Well, I did not deal with the misconceptions the general public may have about indigenous peoples. I just wanted to let the material, i.e. the texts, speak for themselves. I wanted to show how, by studying their poetry, one can appreciate the impressive creativity of these artists, and discover the manner by which, through their art, they are able to influence culture and, therefore, change their own history.

In "Explorations", you discuss how the old tales can vanish from the cultural repertory of some groups because they are no longer performed, while in others, even without being attached to belief in the supernatural, these tales continue to be told as entertainment. What can be done to ensure the oral traditions of our indigenous groups don't just fade away?

To "fade away" and "change" are two different things. I look at cultural change as inevitable; it is the nature of culture, and the nature of human beings, to change and to adapt to historical change. On the level of the texts themselves, it may be said that epics have always existed, both (in our terminology) in prose and in song, or poetry. *Koridos*, once sung, were also told as "fairy tales," as they are today. The context of the performance is the key. Children are told stories, say from the *koridos*, but adults once read these *koridos* (in pamphlet form) and saw them acted out on stage. So while the performance of the stories may change, they may not fade away.

Appendix C:
Interview with Professor
Fernando N. Zialcita

Fernando N. Zialcita is a Professor at the Department of So-ciology and Anthropology of the Ateneo de Manila University, and is the head of its Cultural Heritage Studies Program. He is active in the battle to preserve our cultural identity, particu-larly our intangible heritage. He is also one of the co-authors of the "Soul Book", one of the few attempts made in recent history at a popular introduction to Philippine mythology. He helped organize the Ateneo's "Songs of Memory: International Con-ference on Epics and Ballads", and he graciously allowed me to interview him after the events of the conference.

In the "Soul Book", which you co-authored, the Introduction points out that Filipinos are more familiar with Western my-thology than our indigenous traditions. What do you think could be the reason for this?
There's a lack of interest.

Isn't that because of the lack of knowledge?
It's a chicken-and-egg situation. It's also important to realize that knowing about our creatures of folklore, like the *kapre*, is only a small part. It's lower mythology.

And a lot of that is separate from pre-Hispanic epics, and myths, and the like.
The problem is that when people speak about indigenous culture, some tend to project upon it their fantasies. First you need to understand what indigenous culture looked like. There was more than one culture.

There's a tendency sometimes for people to lump together all the different indigenous mythologies together.
This can be a problem because at any given time different indigenous communities existed at different levels of development. Some communities were more complex. Some were wealthier, whereas those that were poorer would sometimes have simpler mythologies as a result.

I remember that in the "Soul Book", you mentioned that the cosmology grew simpler as one moved North, with less layers present. So, what problems could lumping together mythologies from these different cultures cause?
If you take an anthropologist's point of view, there are all these different ecologies . . . The coastal communities engaged in a lot of trade, so they could be expected to be wealthier than those living in the upland areas, where there's hardly any trade with outsiders. A community with a lot of trade will also have more class stratification, more wealthy people who would also use this wealth in their burial ceremonies . . .

Let me give an example: in Butuan, people are amazed that there is a lot of gold found in burial sites, but this is true for most coastal areas precisely because of trade. Among the Ilongots of Nueva Vizcaya, you'd expect to find less gold in their burial sites.

This would also affect the mythology of these communities. In the coastal areas, there tends to be a belief in the need to bring a retinue of servants to the afterlife. That's why you have instances where *alipin* are buried with their masters. You probably won't find similar mythology in the uplands, where people would not usually be rich enough to command a retinue of servants in life.

So the wealth of the community would be one factor affecting the formation of the mythology. What about contact with outsiders? That too seems to go hand-in-hand with wealth as a consequence of trade.
More foreign elements would enter the mythology in coastal areas, yes. It's a rather complex issue: there are some Islamic elements in the indigenous Tagalog religion as discussed by Father Plasencia—but that's taken for granted because Islam was already here in the sixteenth century.

Given that context, however, what about a non-coastal society such as the Ifugao? We consider the Ifugao—
—relatively isolated.

—yes, and yet they had a rigid class hierarchy. Was wealth the determining factor here? They had gold in their mountains.
The Ifugao had definite stratification because they had wet rice fields. That complicates things. It's not just trade that is a factor—if you have permanent rice cultivation fields, that affects things. If you're practicing shifting cultivation, like the Kalinga who are neighbors of the Ifugao, you'd have less wealth. But permanent fields allows you to have rice harvests that can be stored, and it means that you have land, which leads to a class of people who are really wealthy and that will be reflected in the mythology.

And that's also why rice is so important in their mythology?
Yes. In fact this comes out in [Jules] de Raedt's classic study of religious representations in Northern Luzon. This is a classic example of why it's dangerous to lump mythologies together. According to him, you can actually distinguish between the religions of the peoples in Northern Luzon, in the Cordilleras, who were wet rice cultivators, and those who practiced shifting cultivation.

Those practicing shifting cultivation tend to look at ancestors with fear; they regard their ancestors as the source of sickness. Whereas those practicing white rice cultivation tend to revere their ancestors, and even perform rituals to welcome them. Why is that so? Simply because you cannot have access to land without recourse to your ancestors. In other words, ownership of land was not important for shifting cultivators, but amongst the wet rice cultivators—Ifugao, Bontoc, Kankanay, Nabaloi—land was of major importance, so this gave rise to the practice of ancestor veneration.

Would that be why those societies where land is important also have a tendency to trace their lineage back farther than those, say, in hunting societies?
Yes. It has to do with material things, with land ownership.

So, hypothetically speaking, if we wanted to foster greater understanding of these indigenous religions, what should we do? Teach it by region? Teach a version of these stories earlier in the curriculum, to children? After all, many of these myths were practically bedtime reading in their source communities.
I think you're talking about different problems. If you're talking about reaching a wider audience, what you need are popularizations.

Popularizations though, may at time lead to a certain saniti-zation, as seen with many popularizations of the European Fairy Tales.

I suppose you have to reach the audience at different levels. Sticking to the prose genre, I don't believe there's much harm to a certain sanitization in order to reach a different audience . . . but it is important that the actual source stories be rein-troduced to the audience at a later stage, when they are adults.

Now, that's one part of your question—reaching a wider audience. On the other hand, if what we want is greater intel-ligibility, what you're really talking about is educating adults, or young adults, and I think that for that an eco-systemic regional focus would be very helpful.

Remember, the problem with our educational system is that we try to compress so much into those four years of high school. We want to prepare them for college . . . and yet, right now the first two years of college are basically remedial for high school. If we added those two extra years to High School, we could probably teach much more about the Philippines. And that's important because, as Fr. Nebres has pointed out, Philippine education does not prepare Filipinos to appreciate their own culture. There's not enough Philippine content, and sometimes even that is inaccurate.

The French, who emphasize love for country in their educational system, introduce these aspects in a gradated fashion. In primary school they learn about their localities, their cities or towns, and their traditions. Later they move on to the regional level, and then, finally, the national. If you're growing up as a member of a community, you need to know deeply the traditions of your ancestors.

Isn't an attempt to foster a unified national "identity" one of the reasons why our educational system tries to teach about

the pre-Hispanic "Philippines"—including the diverse mythologies—as a sort of homogenous entity in the first place?
Yes. Some even propose having Bathala stand as a chief god in
a sort of national pantheon that they'd like to construct. But
if you start by emphasizing local knowledge at an early level,
then that could solve the problem.

**While there are people who would "use" mythology, there are,
on the other hand, those who doubt that the study of these old
stories could have any value to them. Why should we study
these myths and legends?**
Let's take the epics, and their heroes—these are important
because they embody the traditional values of an ethnic group.
Even if you don't belong to that ethnic group, it's important
that if you interact with them, you have an understanding
of, for instance, what they view as ideal qualities in men and
women.

**What about those communities who have known nothing but
Catholicism for generations?**
They create their own epics based on these values—take the
Tagalogs, for instance. The *Pasyon* is basically their epic. And
many Catholic communities will still have values influenced
by their epics, whether or not they admit it. The starting point
for anthropologists is that all of us are influenced by our social
contexts. The epics will still inform the culture, even without
being articulated—but there is a need to articulate, because
without that, you don't really know yourself. We cannot assume that we know our social context, or that we have gone
beyond it.

**In one of your other books, "Authentic but Not Exotic", you
wrote about certain misconceptions Filipinos and non-Filipi-**

nos alike have about Filipino culture. What are some of those misconceptions about Philippine mythology and pre-history?
There's a tendency to project monotheism into the past. I doubt many of our ancestors were monotheistic. Let me go back again to the material base of culture. You would expect monotheism to appear in a place where there is centralized authority, since religion is often related to social and political structures. But the pre-Hispanic was very decentralized, many different polities and many different leaders. So monotheism of the Judaic kind would be doubtful, although it is to be expected that some gods would be considered more powerful than others.

But that wouldn't mean that this god could somehow give orders to the other gods.
Right. Of course, there was monotheism with those communities that adhered to Islam, but Islam was only in the Philippines around a century or so earlier than Catholicism, so it's still a "new" religion.

Even given the decentralized nature of the Philippine communities, were there any traits which—while not being universal—were shared amongst some group of these communities? Common characteristics?
Yes, definitely. Many have reverence for spirits of nature, as embodied by objects such as trees that are old and shadowy, like the Balete tree, which is universally revered; unusual rock formations; and the snake, though reverence for the snake is common throughout the world.

What about the idea that people have more than one soul in their bodies?
Yes, that's also prevalent.

Why do you think this concept evolved? It seems easier to envision a unified soul.

This brings us actually to the realm of interpretation. I tend to be rather materialist in my understanding of religion. It all starts with the political economy. I mentioned this in relation to monotheism—it's hard to envision a single leader when all around you see warring communities, for instance.

In the case of the soul, the notion of a unitary conscious-ness, that I myself am responsible for what I've done, this emphasis on the individual . . . that's actually not very common. That only appears at a certain level of development, when there is a legal system and the individual can be held accountable. In traditional societies all over the world, the individual is not the unit of responsibility—the unit of responsibility is often the kin group. So if Malakas has a quarrel with Masigasig, in case of violence it is their kin groups that are held responsible—any member of this kin group can be punished. In that context it's hard to think of an individual as being fully accountable for himself, as a single autonomous unit.

In fact, many of the words that Philippine languages have for "sin" are so . . . strange. "Kasalanan" in Tagalog, or "Basol" in Ilocano . . . they don't imply accountability. They can be used to apply to accidental actions, or mistakes. Neither do they imply something limited to just individuals . . . priests in the past were surprised when Filipinos would go to confession and begin talking about the "kasalanan" of other people.

You mean there was a lack of conception of sin as "punish-ment"? I remember reading something about how there was a common belief that there were simply actions that resulted in bad consequences.

That's true. Look at the Ifugao—there's a spirit for each part of the house, so if you trip on the stairway, it may simply be because the spirit of that part of the stairway is displeased. It may not have been because you did anything wrong—the spirit may simply be capricious. While you can make reparations, it's not because of any individual accountability.

Even in visions of the afterlife, accountability doesn't seem to play a major role. The invisible "tuma" of each man, who knows his deeds in life, is never interrogated about the man's moral qualities, but instead about the number of wives he had...

The afterlife in Philippine mythology usually has nothing to do with sin at all. What matters is your condition when you died—if you died wealthy, you entered the next life rich; if you die a virgin, which was a disgrace, you're a virgin forever. How you died—by a sword, or disease—would also be reflected in your position in the next life.

This brings me back to my point about why Philippine mythology is important. If you try to understand Philippine politics today, part of the problem is lack of accountability. We're still influenced by these early mythologies. Christianity introduced the concept of personal accountability, but we accepted it only on our own terms.

Are there particular myths, or gods, or creatures which you believe, if only they were better known, could capture the imagination of Filipinos?

It's the heroes I'd like to focus on—the gods are a bit too distant for me.

That's fine! There are some gems there. I remember the first time I read about Kudaman and his "giant (pet) bird" which all the ladies seemed to love...

[Laughter] Ah yes, from Palawan. Actually Kudaman's son

was killed accidentally . . . the son found himself underneath the giant bird, which had an erection at the time—and when the pet bird lost its erection, the son was crushed.

Oh man. You can't make this stuff up. Okay, so aside from the usual suspects—Lam-ang, and the rest—are there any heroes which you find particularly interesting?
Aliguyon, of course. His battle with Pumbakhayon was so Filipino—they'd fight fiercely for long periods, then take time-out to eat. Then their mothers intervene, and they become friends at the end and each marries the sister of the other, which is a classic way of ending feuds in the pre-Hispanic Philippines. It's a complete circle.

So with all this good material, why do you think that so few have tried a popular take on the epics and myths, like the "Soul Book"?
People are afraid. What if it doesn't sell? Remember, it's hardly taught in the classroom. There's a curtain of darkness surrounding this particular aspect of our culture.

Which is strange, really, given the periods of "Filipino Pride" that we see on a regular basis…
That's what I mean. We talk about pride in our culture, but often that seems like an empty boast. We don't really know much about it. Sure, certain aspects such as Jose Rizal, the rice terraces, Mayon Volcano . . . I don't see a lot of effort in other areas.

And a lot of that's Luzon-centric.
Yes.

So, what do you think is the state of Philippine pre-Hispanic studies at the moment?

Quite a number of scholars are still involved in the field. Not so many, but quite a number. And some are quite young, like [Philippine ethnomusicologist] Christine Muyco. One reason we organized the "Intangiable Heritage" course in the Ateneo was to encourage students to research the epics. It's not that we're hoping they'll all become experts—hopefully some will—but to open their minds to the existence of these epics, and we provide the [Philippine Epics and Ballads] Archive to provide them access to these stories.

Of course, there's still the lack of entry-level material to contend with. There's a lot of academic material out there now, but these are in journals and specialized publications, and the difficulty is most of our libraries are not well stocked with these, or even with Filipiniana books. Plus, anthropology is not studied much in the Philippines. History, yes, but anthropology, not so much.

Yes, I was surprised by how many of the anthropologists at the conference [the 2011 Songs of Memory International Conference on Epics and Ballads] who specialized in the Philippines were non-Filipinos.

For my final question, I'd just like to ask: do you think that popular fiction could play a role in increasing awareness of our cultural heritage?

I think so. It's worked for Greek mythology.

So, if only more authors would tap into it…

It's a chicken and egg situation again: if they're not exposed to it, then how can they draw from it?

Appendix D:
On Researching Philippine Mythology and Folklore (2021)

I'm no expert on the subject of Philippine Mythology—I'm just an enthusiast. That being said, I do have some experience scrounging around forgotten library shelves in the search for information about Philippine mythology. While by no means a comprehensive guide, here are some tips for the budding researcher. Note that unlike the other parts of this book, I've updated this section for 2021.

It's hard to know where to begin when researching Philippine mythology and folklore. Some of the best introductory materials are out of print, or not readily available. But recently that has begun to change, and I can only hope this trend continues. If Alternative Alamat has awakened a hunger in you to learn more, then allow me to point you to these other titles:

PRIMERS AND OVERVIEWS

"The Soul Book" (GCF Books; 1991) by Fr. Francisco R. Demetrio, Gilda Cordero-Fernando, Fernando N. Zialcita, with art by Roberto Feleo. It's divided into four sections, dealing with pantheons, creation myths, the Babaylan, and the underworld and the layers of the cosmos. Out of print, but copies still occasionally surface. (Its sister title, "The Body Book", has some folktales and beliefs as well.)

"Treasury of Stories" (Anvil Publishing, Inc.; 1995) by E. Arsenio Manuel with Gilda Cordero-Fernando, art by Carlos Valino, Jr. This volume is primarily a compilation of myths, legends, and folktales under different categories such as "Marriage with Celestials" and "Sons of Gods", with commentaries for each category and a brief glossary after each story.

"Outline of Philippine Mythology" (Centro Escolar University Research and Development Center; 1969) by F. Landa Jocano. The book is likely the oldest on this list but is also one of the most detailed. Like the "Treasury of Stories", this book organizes selected myths under different categories: Creation, the Peopling of the World, the Diwata, the Heroes, and Origin Stories. However, a chapter on the "Coming of the Gods" has one of the most complete lists of Philippine deities I've ever come across, particularly when it comes to Tagalog deities, of which so little is known. Long out of print, and I've only seen it at libraries.

The *"Philippine Folk Literature Series"* (University of the Philippines Press; 2001) edited by Damiana Eugenio. The most readily available comprehensive compilation of oral tradition, this series is divided into eight volumes. The first serves as a primer/sampler, with the remaining seven each focusing on a particular topic: Myths, Legends, Folktales, Riddles, Proverbs, Folk Songs, and Epics.

"The Creatures of Philippine Lower Mythology" (Phoenix Publishing House; 1990) by Maximo Ramos. While the books mentioned above provide great overviews, most do not touch upon one of the most beloved aspects of the Philippine supernatural: the kapres, nunos, mangkukulam, and tikbalangs that populate the so-called Lower Mythology. That phrase

has become synonymous with Maximo Ramos, the "Dean of Philippine Lower Mythology", as his books are the leading resource on the topic. One thing to keep in mind about Ramos' books on Lower Mythology is that he frequently re-treads the same ground, but at different levels of complexity. Of those I've read, "The Creatures of Philippine Lower Mythology" is the most detailed, complete with tables of creature characteristics at the end of the book. The most basic is "The Creatures of Midnight" which describes each creature with a short rhyme. Last I checked, you can get copies at the store at Phoenix Publishing House itself.

"Mga Nilalang na Kagila-gilalas" (Adarna House; 2015/2019) by Edgar Calabia Samar, with illustrations by Leo Kempis Ang, Sergio Bumatay III, Mico Dimagiba, JC Galag, Kat Matias, Jap Mikel, Harry Monzon, Stephen Prestado, Conrad Raquel, and Borg Sinaban. Samar is one of the contemporary authors most adept at re-imagining Philippine mythology and folklore in his fiction (his Janus Silang series comes highly recommended). While technically aimed at younger readers, this oversized book (written in Filipino) has a wealth of detail and covers both gods and monsters.

"Ferdinand Blumentritt's Diccionario Mitológico De Filipinas (Dictionary of Philippine Mythology) with English Transla-tions" (The Aswang Project; 2021) The newest addition to this list, this is an English translation of Blumentritt's 1895 work spearheaded by the team at the Aswang Project, a web-site created by Canadian Jordan Clark to serve as an online resource for Philippine folklore.

BOOKS FOR YOUNGER READERS

While the general primers are great introductions to Philippine mythology and folklore, they may not be the best material for younger readers. But in some sense it's the young who should be the primary audience for these old stories, so here are some books which present these stories in a manner accessible to children of different ages.

Tahanan's *"Treasury of Philippine Folk Tales"* series, Anvil's *"Mga Tambay sa Tabi—Tabi"* (Anvil; 2009), and the aforementioned *"The Creatures of Midnight"* are good starting points for younger readers. *"Piagsugpatan: Stories of the Mandaya"* (Adarna House; 2013) by Marcy Dans Lee, is also geared toward younger readers and deals exclusively with tales from the Mandaya.

The compendium books of the Alejandro Pardo series—by Budjette Tan, Kajo Baldisimo, David Hontiveros, Bow Guerrero and Mervin Malonzo—also belong here. These consist of *"The Lost Journal of Alejandro Pardo"* (Summit Books; 2016) and *"The Black Bestiary: An Alejandro Pardo Compendium"* (Summit Books; 2018). These books are thoroughly researched directories of folklore creatures within the framework of a fictional narrative.

REGIONAL FOCUS

The following titles focus on specific cultures or regions, allowing a depth and precision not possible in the more general tomes.

"Epic of Central Panay" series (PUNLAD Research House, Inc.) translated/recorded by F. Landa Jocano.

"Folktales of Southern Philippines" (Anvil Publishing, Inc.; 2011) by Rolando Esteban, Arthur Casanova, Ivie Esteban.

"Voices from Sulu: A Collection of Tausug Oral Traditions" (Ateneo de Manila University Press; 2010) compiled and edited by Gerard Rixhon.

"Oral Literature of the Ifugao" (National Commission for Culture and the Arts; 2005) by Manuel Dulawan.

"An Anthology of Ilianen Manobo Folktales" (San Carlos Publications; 1981) by Hazel J. Wrigglesworth.

"Epics and Ballads of Lam-Ang's Land and People" (UST Publishing House; 2006) recorded/edited by Florentino Hornedo with Saturnino Baltazar.

"El Folk-Lore Filipino" (University of the Philippines Press; 2010) by Isabelo de los Reyes, with English translation by Salud C. Dizon and Maria Elinora Peralta-Imson.

SPECIALIZED TOPICS AND ADVANCED READING

After you've read the more basic texts, or if you're already familiar with Philippine mythology and folklore and would like to read more about specific aspects of it, here are some books that may be worth your while:

"Verbal Arts in Philippine Indigenous Communities" (Ateneo de Manila University Press; 2009) by Hermina Meñez Coben. This book "examines the centrality of verbal art in social life" in ten different Philippine indigenous communities, and in doing so paints a fascinating portrait of the mythologies of

each, and how these are intertwined with their cultures. A bit on the academic side, but the analysis and context Coben provides is invaluable. Her book of essays *"Explorations in Philippine Folklore"* (Ateneo de Manila University Press; 1996) also comes highly recommended.

"Anting-anting: O Kung Bakit Nagtatago sa Loob ng Bato si Bathala" (University of the Philippines Press; 2000) by Nenita Pambid and *"You Shall be as Gods: Anting-anting and the Filipino Quest for Mystical Power"* (Vibal Foundation, Inc.; 2017) are two books that focus on the talismans, amulets, and symbols that have been popular objects of power in the country for centuries.

"Anthology of Asean Literatures: Philippine Metrical Romances" (Nalandangan, Inc.; 1985) edited by Castro, Antonio, Melendrez-Cruz, Mariano, and Makasiar-Puno. Volume 1 deals with indigenous epics from different regions, while Volume 2 compiles Spanish-influenced metrical romances, including Ibong Adarna and Bernardo Carpio.

"Revisiting Usog, Pasma, Kulam" (University of the Philippines Press; 2008) by Michael Tan. The book is an in-depth look at "folk illnesses" and tries categorizing them according to their apparent causes. In the application of social sciences to phenomena such as usog, the book gives us insight into practices of sorcery, and indigenous conceptions of the soul.

"Literature of Voice: Epics in the Philippines" (Ateneo de Manila University Press; 2005) edited by Nicole Revel. Stemming from a 2000 conference of the same name, the book contains various papers on oral tradition/intangible heritage and is notable for coming with a CD (remember those?) that con-

tains recorded excerpts of performances of some of the epics discussed.

"Encyclopedia of Philippine Folk Beliefs and Customs" Volumes 1 and 2 (Xavier University; 1991) by Fr. Francisco Demetrio. Aside from the introduction, the Encyclopedia is less a cohesive book and more a compilation of raw data, listing beliefs and customs revolving around a wide variety of topics, including amulets, diseases, and engkantos.

"May Tiktik sa Bubong, May Sigbin sa Silong" (Ateneo de Manila University Press; 2017), an anthology edited by Allan N. Derain, and *"The Aswang Inquiry"* (GCF Books; 1998) by Frank Lynch, S.J. with illustrations by Gilda Cordero-Fernando, both focus on one kind of folklore creature, the aswang.

ONLINE ACADEMIC RESOURCES

There are now a number of websites, youtube channels, and podcasts that cover Philippine myth and folklore. I would like to give special mention here to two of the most important academic resources available online: the Philippine Epics and Ballads Archive of the Ateneo de Manila University (epics.ateneo.edu/epics/) and the archives of the Philippine Studies: Hisotical and Ethnographic Viewpoints journal (philippinestudies.net).

Appendix E:
Glossary of Selected Terms

Adobo: Encompasses a wide variety of dishes, where meat or seafood is marinated in a sauce of vinegar and garlic, and cooked until brown.

Alimuom: The smell that accompanies the release of heat from the soil after rainfall.

Aswang: Either a reference to one of four types of demons from Philippine folklore, or a general term for "monster".

Baybayin: A system of writing practiced in some areas of the Philippines before the Spanish colonization; the word means "to spell out in syllables".

Datu: The general term for the chief or head of a community in the Philippines, particularly in the Visayas region, before the Spanish colonization.

Indio: The Spanish term for the people native to the islands of the Spanish Philippines.

Kaluluwa: A Filipino word that roughly approximates "soul" or spirit."

Kapre: A generally benevolent demon from Philippine folklore. While it is human-like in appearance, it is characterized by great height, a hairy body, and its habit of smoking cigars.

Karibang: A dwarfen creature from Philippine mythology.

Manang: A term of respect, used to refer to an older woman.

Tikbalang: A demon from Philippine folklore, with the head and legs of a horse, and the body of a man. It is said to take joy in causing mischief for humans, usually by impersonating a relative and leading them astray on a journey.

Tutong: Used to refer to the hard, crusted rice found at the bottom of a pot, after cooking; the word itself means "toasted".

Yaya: A nanny; a maid with the primary responsibility of caring for the children of a family.

Upo

Andrew Drilon

Andrew Drilon has been telling stories through the medium of comics for almost a decade now. He first ventured into the realm of prose fiction in order to improve his abilities as a comics writer, and quickly found himself enamored by the form. Since then, his short stories have been published both locally and internationally. He was a finalist for the Philippine Free Press Literary Awards and is the recipient of a Philippine Graphic/ Fiction Award. Andrew is currently at work on his first original graphic novel, Black Clouds.

This six page comic is based on the story "All-Head Juan" in Maximo Ramos' Tales of Long Ago in the Philippines (Phoenix Publishing 1990). Andrew reworked the story to de-Christianize it and make it more of a pre-Hispanic tale. The art, according to Andrew, draws from the work of Francisco V. Coching, particularly his "Lapu-Lapu" run in Pilipino Komiks.

Published by Tuttle Publishing, an imprint of Periplus Editions (HK) Ltd.

www.tuttlepublishing.com

Library of Congress Control Number: 2022932075

ISBN 978-0-8048-5557-0

Distributed by

North America, Latin America & Europe
Tuttle Publishing
364 Innovation Drive
North Clarendon
VT 05759-9436 U.S.A.
Tel: 1 (802) 773-8930
Fax: 1 (802) 773-6993
info@tuttlepublishing.com
www.tuttlepublishing.com

Asia Pacific
Berkeley Books Pte. Ltd.
3 Kallang Sector #04-01
Singapore 349278
Tel: (65) 6741-2178
Fax: (65) 6741-2179
inquiries@periplus.com.sg
www.tuttlepublishing.com

Japan
Tuttle Publishing
Yaekari Building 3rd Floor
5-4-12 Osaki Shinagawa-ku
Tokyo 141 0032
Tel: (81) 3 5437-0171
Fax: (81) 3 5437-0755
sales@tuttle.co.jp
www.tuttle.co.jp

25 24 23 22
5 4 3 2 1   2204TO
Printed in Malaysia

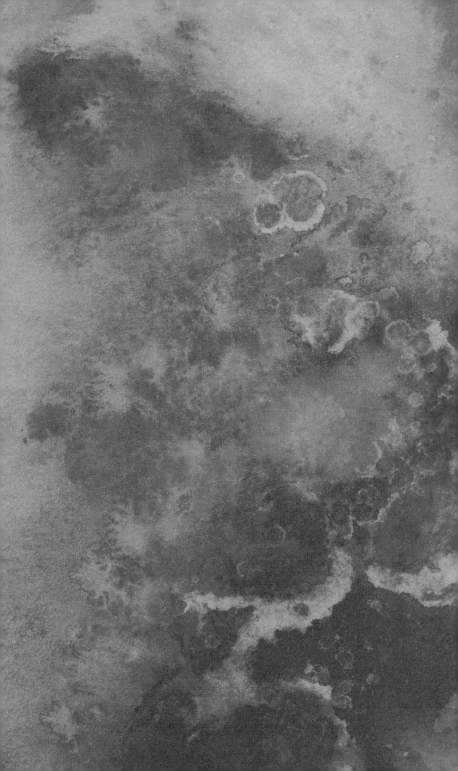